Broken Mirror
and other morbid tales

featuring the novella ~ Basement Beauty

Carmilla Voiez

Cover art by: Nicola Ormerod
Edited by: Vanessa Knipe
Poetry for Basement Beauty written by: Glen W Hunter.

This is a work of fiction. All of the characters, organizations and events portrayed in this novel are a product of the author's imagination. Any resemblance to persons, living or dead, actual events, or organizations is entirely coincidental.

2nd edition

The trigger warnings are not designed as spoilers. Their purpose is to warn people, suffering from PTSD due to events in their own lives, so they can avoid those situations in fiction that may send them spiralling back to a place and time they have worked hard to escape. Or so they can decide when and where they feel strong enough to confront deep fears through fiction. This collection includes some stories which contain descriptions of violence, mental illness, sexual assault, self-harm, body dysmorphia and bullying. Trigger warnings for each relevant tale will be as accurate and comprehensive as possible.

While some of these stories show acts of violence by people with mental illness, figures clearly show that such people are far more likely to be victims of violence than perpetrators.

I hope you enjoy the collection and remember that it is designed as entertainment for the brave and foolhardy.

Other books by Carmilla Voiez

<u>Novels</u>

The Ballerina and the Revolutionary
The Starblood Trilogy -

> Book 1 – Starblood
> Book 2 – Psychonaut
> Book 3 – Black Sun

<u>Graphic Novels</u>

Starblood , with art by Anna Prashkovich
Psychonaut, with art by Anna Prashkovich

<u>Short Stories</u>

The Erotic Tales of Carmilla Voiez
Carmilla has contributed short stories, some of which have been reproduced in this collection, to a number of anthologies.
Find out more at - www.carmillavoiez.com

Table of Contents

Dedicated to

Glen - my muse and my comfort; Vanessa – my friend, aide and editor; Nicola – my friend, advisor and cover maker; and David – my father and mentor.

Thank you to everyone who has supported and loved me including my amazing and often patient daughters who are still too young to read this collection, Andrew, Ann, Sarah and Colleen.

Regency Heights (Salon of Lost Souls) was, in part, inspired by the beautiful Duff House in Scotland.

Basement Beauty

TW: Kidnapping and imprisonment

~ 1 ~

'You're too beautiful to be killed, Tay,' Lynsey assured her, brushing a manicured hand through freshly lightened hair.

'What the fuck do you mean?' Amalthea shook her head, jostling afro curls and revealing a petulant frown that drew her plump cheeks inwards.

'Aint you heard? All the victims were ugly. Aint gonna happen to you, kiddo.'

Amalthea gazed at the empty pint glass in her hands. 'Ugly?'

'Yeah, not grotesque freaks or anything, just plain ugly: big noses, crooked teeth, greasy hair, you know. When I went to the dentist this morning they told me everyone and their f'in dog's booked in for cosmetic work.'

'Isn't that odd?' Amalthea rotated the glass this way and that between caramel fingers.

Lynsey shrugged. 'Dunno.'

'I think it's odd.'

'Whatever, girl. Just stop stressing, okay. You're too beautiful to die.'

Amalthea glanced over the bar at the almost empty nightclub. 'Seems quiet tonight.'

'Yeah, well it's still early. Heard there's a gig on. Lots of people probably there. They'll lurch in here eventually.' Lynsey wiped down the dark wood counter with a damp, blue cloth.

'Hope so. Drags when it's this quiet.' Amalthea placed the clean glass on a shelf at knee level. 'Makes me want to open a book.'

Lynsey nodded. 'Why don't you? Hey, you alright for a minute if I pop out for a ciggie?'

Amalthea nodded toward the dimly lit room and grimaced. 'Uh yeah. I think I can manage these three alone.'

'Cheers, babes.' Lynsey kissed Amalthea's cheek and exited through a door between rows of optics.

Amalthea dried another glass from the crate and set it on the shelf. She repeated the action until the crate was empty without being disturbed by customers. When she looked up again she noticed a young man had entered the club and was strolling towards her. She recognised him from poetry nights. As always, he arrived alone. This evening he carried a slender book. She tried to see the cover, but it was angled away from her.

'Hi,' she said as he sat on a stool.

He smiled warmly. He was pretty, for a white boy. His skin seemed to have the soft glow of health that was rare in young men from this Scottish city. He reminded Amalthea of the father she hadn't seen in over a decade, except this lad was even paler and his eyes resembled emeralds held in front of a flame.

'Coffee, please.'

Amalthea nodded. She had never known him to order alcohol. Most of the patrons were ardent drinkers and this boy… man stood out for his lack of inebriation. Was he was still too young to drink or was he a recovering alcoholic? Would he frequent a club if he had a drinking problem? It was more likely that he simply found other ways to relax - those words clutched in his hand or the ones in his head? He fascinated her, although she wasn't sure why. Physically, sexually, he wasn't her type at all, but there was something about his gentle calm that attracted her and what better time to strike up a conversation than a quiet night like this?

She switched on the coffee machine and poured in freshly ground beans.

'Seems quiet,' he said.

'Very,' she answered. 'What brings you here tonight? I normally just see you on poetry nights.'

'You notice?' he asked and his eyes gleamed brighter.

She stepped back and swallowed. Not another one? This club was full of would-be creeps and admirers. It was often hard to tell the difference between the two from this side of the bar. She hastily backtracked. 'Sure. I know all my regulars. Do you write poetry?'

'I'm not sure it's any good.'

'Ahhh, you should perform a piece here one night. It's a friendly crowd. They won't bite.'

He laughed. 'Yeah, maybe. It could be fun to perform for… everyone, I guess. Do you write?'

'Prose,' she answered. 'Nothing published. What book is that?'

'Not mine. I've not been published either. A bit of Plath.' He flashed the cover at her.

'You like Sylvia Plath?'

'I guess I have a thing for desperate sorrow.' His face flushed and he suddenly appeared vulnerable.

She nodded, warming to him again. 'There's a lot of that in this town.'

'I'm Daniel.' He extended his exquisitely manicured right hand towards her.

Her hand met his half way across the bar. Her chewed fingernails, chipped purple polish and brown skin made an interesting contrast, worker versus what - public school boy, intellectual, rich kid? He seemed so different to her and yet the same. It confused her. It always did when she met people from such different backgrounds with a shared love of words. 'Amalthea,' she said. 'Or Tay.'

'Delighted to make your acquaintance, Amalthea. Do you work here every night?'

'Almost.'

The machine's noise altered as the dripping coffee filled a cream-coloured mug. She passed Daniel a black coffee with no sugar - his usual order.

'Thank you.' He nodded and took a sip. 'And what do you do when you aren't here?'

'Sleep, write, oh and I'm studying English at the Uni.'

'Busy...' He seemed pensive for a moment. He teetered on the edge of something. Whatever it was, he decided not to ask. Instead he stood up and picked up his mug. 'Thank you, Taya,' he said and walked to a leather chair below a green spotlight.

Lynsey bustled back through the door, dragging cold air and the stench of tobacco with her. 'Did I miss anything?'

'Not much. I put the glasses away and we have a new customer.'

Lynsey stared across at Daniel and exhaled. 'Seen him before, a bit of an odd ball, quiet, always alone.'

Amalthea nodded. 'Maybe that's the way he likes it.'

~ 2 ~

Amalthea stood outside the unlit entrance to The Pit and breathed in the cool, pre-dawn air. One hand brushed wild curls from her mouth and tucked them behind her ear. They sprang back across her cheek immediately, untameable.

As her skin acclimatised she drew jacket sleeves over her arms. A movement at the edge of her vision attracted her attention and she peered towards the shadowy alley where the night club bins were stored. Her direct gaze didn't reveal any ghoul, goblin, animal or person skulking in the darkness, watching and waiting for her to leave, but her mind created a sinister shape anyway. For the past six weeks the evening news had continually reported unnatural deaths city-wide. Rumours of a modern day Jack the Ripper were rife. Now every alleyway had become hostile territory and every shadow a killer, preparing to strike.

With her meditative moments, of simply being, stolen by fear of the impenetrable darkness, Amalthea decided to button her coat and get moving. Home wasn't far away, a mere ten minute walk and at four in the morning most of the drunks were already home, sleeping it off, or standing, unsteadily in taxi queues, waiting for chariots to return them safely to their beds. That was one thing to be said about fear of what might lurk the dark - it was good for the economy.

Gentle but pervasive drizzle vainly attempted to flatten her hair. Street lights mutated into dancing constellations and pavements were dotted with quicksilver puddles. Amalthea's boots leaked and the liquid made her toes squelch. Sucking and dripping sounds masked the noise of her footsteps and the perfectly matched slapping of shoe leather behind her. Of course, when she glanced back, the street was empty, but the moment she faced forwards she felt his presence behind her, as always, matching her stride. He was the shadow from which she fled, unseen but perceived through all her other senses, making her hairline tingle - the man who wasn't there.

She had tried to tell Lynsey of this consuming fear, but her friend hadn't understood, dismissing her fears as paranoia. She decided in the future to only mention this deep, primal knowledge to her diary and wondered for one terrifying moment whether his other victims had known they were being hunted, but had kept silent or were disbelieved until the moment their vacated shells were discovered. She considered why she had dogmatically given this disembodied threat a male gender then shook her head. It was perfectly natural; serial killers were almost always male, weren't they? *The one who kills me will probably be male too*, she reasoned.

Her scalp itched. Realising the utter pointlessness of another backwards glance, she balled her fists and marched onwards. Just five more minutes and she could lock the darkness outside, for what that was worth.

A shriek broke through the pittering-pattering shroud of raindrops. It echoed between tall Victorian town houses, converted into flats and bedsits - a cat or a baby waking from a nightmare? She waited for a repeat of the noise until she became aware that she had stopped moving and was standing as still as a statue as the rain continued to fall around and upon her. The sound didn't return. Shivering, she willed her right foot to make its journey, one step forwards and asked her hip to tilt and her knee to bend. Movement didn't follow her commands so she concentrated on her left foot instead - still nothing. Swallowing hard, she wiggled the toes of her left foot. Water moved between skin and cotton; the sensation made her nauseous.

'Just walk, Tay,' she whispered.

Rain hissed in her ears. Beneath her chin a waterfall tumbled onto her chest.

'Just walk… five minutes!'

Ahead of her a tree that overhung the path shook water from its leaves like a huge dog. Large drops splattered as they hit the ground. What waited beyond that tree, hidden behind the trunk? She considered taking a longer route home where the streets were less shadowy and the traffic more regular.

Shivering from cold and fear, she watched as the heavy branches bent and purged until the urge to vomit returned. One hand stretched out to a rough red-brick wall beside her, knees bent and hips angled yet her feet remained bolted to the spot.

How many had been killed already this year - ten, no twelve, would she be the thirteenth? She shook her head;

this fear was not rational. She wasn't being hunted and her home was a mere five minute walk from this spot. Five minutes… she could walk for five minutes. Five minutes… no distance at all, yet one step forwards felt beyond her reach.

'Tay, get a grip!' Her mind used her mother's voice, dominant, matriarchal and full of a rich, musical patois. She nodded, fighting her foolishness and the paralysing fear of what - a tree, a shadow and a lone shriek? What set her off this time? 'You is fierce, a powerful woman. This shit is beneath you, Amalthea. You shame me.'

Amalthea pushed against the wall, straightening her hips and knees. Raising her head, she blinked diamonds from her eyes. The raindrops altered their route and formed puddles within the cradles of her earlobes. With Herculean effort, she stepped forward. Once freed from their traps her legs adopted their natural rhythm. Swift and sure she passed beneath the branches as a single sphere fell and trickled between her neck and jacket collar. In less than five minutes she reached home, pushing bolts into place and turning keys in locks.

The breath she took filled her lungs with warm, dry air. She gulped it down as though it was her first breath then headed for the bathroom and a towel.

~ 3 ~

'I heard there was another one last night,' Lynsey said.

They stood together, behind the bar, scanning the room. Another night another dollar.

'Another murder?' Amalthea asked. 'Does that make it thirteen now?'

'Yes and they still don't have a clue who's doing it. Is my makeup okay? How about my hair? I could do with going to the stylist again, really, but it's so expensive.'

'You look fine.'

'I wonder whether they all thought that? And I know I could do with losing a few pounds. Oh stop sneering, Amalthea. The latest victim is another woman. That's eight women and five men. Do you think he prefers women? Do you think the men were accidents? The last five have all been women, right?'

Amalthea shrugged. 'I don't know, Lynsey.'

'Don't walk home alone tonight. Promise me,' Lynsey said.

'I thought you said I was too beautiful to die.'

'Just in case. You know, the fear in this city is growing. People are talking about setting up vigilante groups as the police can't seem to do anything. It's going to get really bad. I can feel it in my stomach.'

Amalthea shook her head. 'I can't afford a taxi and

I've got no one to walk with.'

'How about if I stay back tonight. Give you a lift home.'

'What about your kids?'

'I can be late for one night,' Lynsey assured her.

'Then what about tomorrow and the next night and the night after that?'

'Maybe they'll catch him.'

Amalthea doubted it. 'You think?'

'No, but each day at a time, right? Stay alive today and let tomorrow take care of itself.'

'Seems pointless.'

'Isn't everything when you analyse it. Come on. For me. Let me drive you home.'

'Honestly, Lynsey, there's no need.'

Lynsey patted Amalthea's arm. 'I don't want to walk to the car park alone.'

Amalthea exhaled loudly then nodded. 'Sure. It'd be great if you dropped me home tonight. I'd feel much safer.'

'Thanks, babes. I wonder if it'll be busy tonight.'

'Maybe people are staying indoors.' Amalthea shuddered as coldness gripped her limbs.

'Don't blame them. I would if I could. Do you think they'll set a curfew?'

'What? The police? Shit, I hope not. I'll be screwed. How will I pay rent?'

'Well, it's only eight o'clock. I guess it's too early to panic about the emptiness. Wish we had something on tonight though. Something to attract the punters away from their TV sets and out into the frosty night.' Lynsey chewed a nail then stopped and stared at her fingers. She rubbed the slightly chipped polish, frowning. 'Dammit.'

At the end of the quiet night, the tills were emptied and the safe filled. Amalthea locked the back door behind them. Lynsey interlocked her arm with Amalthea's. 'Your carriage awaits, Ma'am.'

They hurried towards the car park. Rain fell from the starless sky. Mist obscured the street lights and the air was chill. The Mini with its super heating system beckoned them and they rushed towards it arm in arm.

Other than Lynsey's, only one car remained in the car park. It was at the far side, at least twenty metres away from them and it appeared empty.

The two friends almost fell through the doors into the low seats. 'Mmmmm,' Lynsey said.

Amalthea nodded. 'Thanks for the lift.'

'Thanks for walking with me to the car.'

'No problem at all,' Amalthea replied.

Lynsey switched on the lights, put the car into gear and drove away. Neither of them noticed that the lights of the other car switched on or that a large, dark vehicle followed them out of the compound.

~ 4 ~

'This was left for you,' Gareth said, handing Amalthea an envelope the moment she arrived at The Pit for her shift.

'Who's it from?' she asked.

'Damned if I know. Open it and find out.'

'Did you see who left it?'

'No it was stuffed through the letter box this morning.'

Amalthea studied the sealed envelope then wandered off.

'Not going to share the secret with me, then?' Gareth asked.

'Not this time,' she answered.

'Oh, Lynsey phoned. Kid's sick. I'd stay but I have a thing later. Will you be okay?'

'Who else is coming in?' Amalthea called over her shoulder.

'Jamie and Steve at ten.'

'Friday. Band night. Might be a bit tight. What time are you leaving?'

'Not until eleven.'

'Jamie and Steve staying til the end?'

'Yup.'

'We'll manage. You do your thing.'

'Awesome! Don't stress about tidying the place. The cleaners are in tomorrow morning anyway. Just cash up and get your ass home.'

'Will do.' Amalthea tore open the envelope. Inside was a scribbled note. "Meet me, Friday at eleven at The Arches"

'What is it?' Gareth asked.

'Nothing,' Amalthea answered, rolling the paper into a tight ball and stuffing it into her jeans pocket.

Amalthea was so busy behind the bar she didn't even have chance to say goodbye to her boss when he left. Luckily Jamie and Steve worked hard and no customer was ignored. The music was mellow and rocky, not Amalthea's taste, but pleasant enough. At least it wasn't ear-splitting punk. Some Fridays she wished she could wear ear-plugs, but having attempted it once she found herself unable to grasp customers' orders properly and quickly gave up on the whole idea. Even so, walking home in the middle of the night, ears ringing in a tone she would never hear again, wasn't her idea of a good time. When she told Gareth he laughed through a sympathetic mask, but hadn't promised any changes in the line-up. One day she would leave and that would show him, or else he'd simply hire another student who would continue doing all the crappy jobs she did and he wouldn't miss her at all.

Eleven o'clock passed without incident and it was half-past when Amalthea next checked her watch. She hadn't been planning to attend the rendezvous, meeting strangers in quiet streets was even less fun than letting punk rock destroy your hearing, but she did feel that she should have acknowledged the invitation in some way at the designated time. She decided to forget about it. If someone needed to speak with her they would find another way.

She dried a hot pint glass and popped it onto the rack to cool. 'I'd better collect glasses,' Amalthea said, tapping Jamie on the shoulder.

Jamie nodded. 'Hurry back.'

Amalthea weaved between bodies. That night the club was full of grungy student types with dirty jeans and oily hair. Many of the men were unshaven, rough stubble not beards, threatening to scratch anyone who dared get too close. They reminded Amalthea of cacti, look but don't touch.

She hurried around the club, laden with empties, careful not to drop any or knock into the customers. It was a talent she had honed over the months and tonight it served her well. She returned to the bar red-faced and breathless, but without breaking a single glass.

'Glad you're back. Could do with a hand,' Jamie said.

'Where's Steve?'

'The band needed help with the sound system. He'll

be right back.'

'Okay. Sorry I took so long.'

The patrons grumbled. They did not like to wait for their alcoholic refreshments. Amalthea shifted up a gear and cleared the queue before Steve returned.

'You're a whizz,' Jamie said.

'Umm, is that a good thing?'

'Absolutely.'

~ 5 ~

Daniel stroked the thick, dark hair of a woman as she nestled her face in his lap. Her flesh was covered in goose bumps. He cupped her chin and lifted her face so that her glassy eyes stared blankly in the general direction of his face. He searched for her wild spirit, crouching somewhere behind that expressionless face.

Her neck was bruised purple and green. Red juice, from the strawberries he fed her, dripped down her chin. He smudged it around her mouth with his thumb, licking his lips as the heat of his desire rose once again. She didn't react to the change in his body, the hardness, almost as if it was his warmth and strength she craved rather than his sex. Playfully he tugged her hair until she yelped, softly. As her body relaxed the dull thud of metal against stone resonated through the cellar. She peered up at him and the chain rose with her, the chain he had attached to the metal collar around her throat.

He remembered when he met Emily; she'd been dancing, magnificent in her graceful movements. She was fiercely exciting, playful and intelligent. Qualities she'd long since buried.

Amalthea's face filled his thoughts. Perhaps she was the one, the one who might truly love him as an equal?

'Would you like a new playmate?' he asked.

Her eyes darkened, in anger or jealousy, he wasn't sure which.

'Tell me what you want, Emily.'

'I want to go home.' Her voice was a whisper, unused to speaking and terrified to be heard. 'Please, let me go home.'

'You know I can't do that, Emily.'

'Then kill me, drain me. I can't… don't make me… set me free, please.'

'I won't drink from you, Emily.'

'Why? I know what you are, what you do… I know what you want.'

Daniel shook his head. 'You're so wrong. That isn't what I want.'

'But I've seen you.'

He stroked her hair. 'I won't ever hurt you, Emily. I promise.'

She shuddered under his caresses. 'Why am I here? What do you want from me?'

'I love you.'

She spat at him. 'You call this love?'

Daniel's hand moved and Emily crawled into the shadows as far away from him as her chain would allow. He knelt beside her and stroked her cheek. She shuddered again. Fear drained from her eyes and she became empty, void of all emotion. She was never there when he kissed her or touched her with a tenderness he was certain she would enjoy if she only allowed herself to experience it. He held his arms open for her. 'At least let me warm you.'

She nodded and moved closer. 'You could give me clothes,' she whispered.

His arms encircled her cold, damp body. So fragile in his arms, he feared she was losing too much weight. 'You should eat more. Don't you like the food I give you?'

She didn't answer. Her cheek rested against his chest, where his heartbeat might have been if he was human.

'I do love you,' he told her, stroking and untangling her hair again. 'I wish you could see that.'

She didn't challenge him that time. Her body felt limp against his and he realised she had fallen asleep. He stood up, cradling her in his arms like a baby. A soft mattress with angora blankets and silk sheets butted up against whitewashed stones. He laid her on it and reclined beside her, one hand supporting his cheek and the other resting on her tiny waist. He kissed her brow and pulled the luxurious covers over her flesh then arranged the chain so she was unlikely to entangle herself if she moved in her sleep.

When Emily and he were first courting, their conversations had stimulated him beyond all measure. How could loving a mind as fine as hers be wrong? Even after years of psychoanalysis, he still couldn't see a beautiful human face without wanting to kiss it. Their body parts fitted perfectly and while they were unable to procreate it was insane to believe that sex was merely a tool for making babies. If he could explain it to the others... but that was impossible when every relationship with a human ended like this - a chained, half-starved body in the basement, the potential never fulfilled, the love never returned, the flame of desire extinguished before it had time to light the shadows of his soul.

His love for them damned him and he knew that as well as anyone.

But he couldn't change what he wanted; he only wished it was possible to make those he desired want him too, even when they discovered his nature. Perhaps Amalthea would be different. She was strong, exciting, dominant and confident. She might be the one person in the whole filthy world able to heal him, change him and help him to show his family why a human was worth love too.

He would recite poetry for Amalthea. Human women fell in love so easily with language. The right words whispered in an ear sent shivers of pleasure across flesh. How in touch with their longing humans were. Perhaps that was why their lives were so short. If they lived for hundreds of years, the impact they had on the world and each other would be immeasurable. The thought excited him, taboo though it was.

Vampires had achieved so little of note over the millennia that their history books were mere pamphlets. Where were the DaVincis and the Shakespeares of his species? Longevity was a curse, delaying every action for want of any sense of urgency. There was no need to create something to outlive you when you expected to live forever. Only science attracted the minds of vampires, mostly in order to perfect a vampire master race and eradicate heterogeneity. Perhaps, more than longevity that was the curse of the vampires – that they were all expected to think alike and act alike. Art could never thrive in such a stifling environment.

Leaving Emily to her dreams, he returned upstairs. He pulled out a photograph and a pad of writing paper from the desk in his study. The picture was of Amalthea, standing outside the door to The Pit, eyes half closed, completely at peace with herself. He envied her stillness and the way she seemed complete within her own skin. She was magnificent.

He picked up a pen and allowed the nib to hover just above the paper. *What should I write?* It needed to be personal, from the heart. It needed to resonate within her as something she would wish to say to a lover and yearn to hear.

"Amalthea, you enchant me. I want to know what hides behind your smile. You are everything that is good in this world and you deserve the purest love imaginable. Meet me when your shift ends and I will gladly show you what you mean to me. Eternally yours, Daniel."

He folded the letter into a rich plum-coloured envelope and scribed her name upon it before retiring to his bedroom. Humans were not like vampires. Their feelings were complex and tainted by fear of their mortality. They entered wholeheartedly into love affairs. It was their way of staying ahead of death. In contrast vampire love seemed transitory and hollow, meaningless. Simply a source of physical pleasure and occasionally procreation, not the life affirming, spiritual ecstasy he witnessed among those humans lucky enough to find the one or ones they loved.

If his pets had failed to deliver on this unspoken promise, perhaps it was because sex with him brought death a step closer rather than pushing it away; maybe they knew this instinctively and maybe Amalthea would too. He hoped not, but prepared himself for yet another disappointment.

It had taken years to understand that these women,

who seemed so loving at first, might choose to betray him and leave. That he kept them imprisoned was their fault rather than his and he wished they shared this house properly with him. It would please him greatly to tuck each one into their bed at night. If only they might understand that he was no threat to them, but they were blind to his love and devotion, heartless and careless of his desires. It made him sad, but it was better than living without their company.

He prepared dinner, filled four glasses with wine and took it all into the cellar. A bare light bulb made the space appear bright and soulless. He placed a plate and glass in front of Emily. Grunting, she sat up. Moving further into the maze of rooms and corridors, he took food and wine to the other women.

Diane had been a waitress in a coffee shop where he used to hang out and watch hipsters drink lattes and plan their lives. He offered to walk her home one evening when her shift ended. Her smile was warm and intelligent, but she didn't smile for him anymore and she hardly moved when he placed her dinner in front of her mattress. He stroked her hair, trying to wake her, but she seemed deep in some dream. He hoped it was a good one.

Charlie had been an exotic dancer. He'd seen a poster featuring her outside a strip club in Soho. She had lived with him for two years and her once plump figure had all but vanished over that time. Her arms were now defined only by narrow bones. 'Please eat,' he whispered as he placed his offering before her. Her green eyes flickered open, but there was no trace of recognition in her stare. He touched her hair and moved on.

Finally he reached Moira, remembering how he met her in a library. She had so many books that she hardly had the strength to carry them to her car. He helped her, then watched the library for three weeks until she returned. It was Moira who had first sparked his interest in poetry. She loved the romance of language and the more expert he became in its use the more she fell in love with him. The first time they made love she cried. She said he was beautiful and made him believe it. They lived happily together for three months until she found the key to his cellar. In the end he had to slap her when hysteria threatened to choke her. She fell to the floor, hitting her head on the edge of a table and from that moment she hadn't spoken a word to him. He no longer felt beautiful when she looked at him. Now he felt like a monster. He blindfolded her so he no longer saw his reflection in her pale blue eyes. When he left her food he placed a spoon within her palm and directed her hand to the plate. She never removed the cloth from her eyes. Perhaps she was more comfortable in the dark or perhaps seeing him was too terrible for her to bear.

He'd had other pets before these. In one week he lost an entire batch to flu. He'd mopped their brows and fed them penicillin, but they never recovered their appetites even when their fevers broke. Heartbroken, he vowed never to take another woman home, but six weeks later he was out hunting again, searching for another pretty face and clever mind with whom to spend his evenings. It was an addiction, but there were no self-help groups for people like him.

He wandered back through the cellar, past Charlie who was ignoring the platter completely in favour of some dream and past Diane who had woken and was playing listlessly with her food. As he reached the corner, he slipped and barely recovered his footing. He clung to the wall for support. Wet, warm and sticky, it coated his skin in delicious, sensual ways. Everything was red. He wondered for a moment whether he was sick; sometimes he forgot to feed for too long and a crimson mania came upon him. He put his hand to his forehead and his palm slid against the skin as if oiled. Red covered his fingers and spread out below his feet, seeping across the room. The wall was dotted with it. He knew the smell immediately and like any great connoisseur he knew the vintage. He didn't need to taste it to know, even so he sucked it from the tip of his index finger. A ripe, earthy jus with tangy head notes of iron, Emily's blood.

He followed the trail to a slumped body and gathered her in his arms. On the ground in front of her, glass shards glinted in an ocean of blood. Her wrists and throat had been sliced and her heartbeat silenced, but on her face was a smile that chilled him more than the vision of her splattered blood. It was a smile of relief, pleased to be free at last. He held her closer and wept.

While he mourned, he cleaned her flesh with his tongue. He saw himself as she had always seen him, a monster.

~ 6 ~

He cleaned his skin and changed his clothes before returning to Diane's chamber. She was still asleep and hadn't touched her food, so he left it there for her. Moira was finishing her meal.

'Hello Moira.'

She lifted her head.

'I've written a new poem. Would you like to hear it?' She nodded and he recited it for her.

'I gave her my heart after years of promises

and she ran screaming from the room as it pulsed in my hand

I couldn't understand why it didn't go as planned

Maybe my love was too literal

Visceral and exposed like a raw nerve

Too quick to serve myself to her this way

I've always been too impulsive

Quick to follow my sorrow down the wrong street
The sound of feet
Running
Charging
Headlong into memories lane down a soon forgotten
path
A run-down, ransacked and rancid math
of you subtracted from me
equalling nothing but fractions and remainders
but these are the dangers of Cupid's bow
Love will come
Love will grow
Love will go
or wither on the vine
In this green house of time there are many dead roses.'

The words trickled into her consciousness and he saw pleasure in her face. When he finished he kissed her dry lips. 'I miss you,' he told her. He stroked her blindfold and she quivered slightly. 'Shall I take this off?'

She shook her head, defiantly. 'I cannot look at you.' The words sounded cracked and broken, like her lips. They chilled him.

'Why?' he asked.

'Because the fire of my hatred will consume us both,' Moira replied.

He hung his head and blinked away tears. 'I'm sorry.'

'Not sorry enough,' she rasped.

He sat beside her in silence.

'I can smell blood on you,' she said. 'Whose blood is it?'

He shook his head before realising she couldn't see him.

He took Charlie's and Moira's empty dishes with him as he climbed the stairs. The space Emily had left mocked him, knowing the only impact his removal from this world would have on anyone was a sense of relief. Even Charlie, Moira and Diane, although they would probably starve, would see his absence as a blessing - a chance to fade into dust.

None of it was fair. He was good. Better than most of his kind. When he killed he beautified his prey. He gave them a luminescence and mystery in death that they lacked in life. He killed the most clumsy, the most ugly humans he found then made them precious, creating statues of their cold flesh. It was his gift to humanity. He gave them beauty. He wished his own kind could see that. If only they'd open their minds and appreciated his art. He might been a renegade, but he was still one of them, and their absence in his life created a lonely void that human women filled.

Restlessly, he wandered through empty rooms. Sleep seemed far from his grasp and his body and mind were agitated. The frustrating inaction, always hiding from sight and the sickening cowardice he maintained to survive, did not feel comfortable. It was a chain around his neck, trapping him in circumstance as surely as the women below his feet.

Would tonight change anything for him? He considered again the pros and cons of meeting Amalthea outside The Pit as planned. The temptation to throw his self, body and soul, at her rose, but he tamped it down. Such actions, perfectly acceptable, even expected amongst his own kind, frightened human females. With them more subtlety was required. He found himself, mentally debating every choice, every move he made before he made it. Perhaps by desiring humans he was simply exchanging one set of rules that had been etched onto his skin by centuries of training, for others that were alien and confusing. That was what frustrated him most, his lifestyle was not the easy choice; it was hard and full of challenges from every direction. What fool could think he would ever choose to be this way or be taught to be something different?

To-ing and Fro-ing between going or staying, he hovered in the hallway, clutching his car keys. His posture screamed tension, shoulders hunched and raised almost to the bottom of his earlobes, hands in fists, knees locked. A thousand voices rushed around his mind advising different courses of action. He wanted to drown them out but they persisted. Unable to stand this stasis any longer, he fled the house, started his car and headed towards Glasgow and Amalthea.

~ 7 ~

'Hi, Taya,' Daniel said as she reached the corner.

Amalthea jumped.

'I'm sorry,' he said. 'I've scared you. Did you get my letter?'

She nodded, clenching her jaw. She suspected that she must have appeared comical, but Daniel didn't laugh. *What the fuck?*

'You're in danger,' he told her.

She shook her head. 'I won't let you hurt me,' she growled.

'Not from me.' He stretched his palms towards her and knelt on the wet pavement in supplication. 'I don't want to hurt you.'

She glared at him, silently, her eyes full of mistrust. *Fuck you! Get out of my life!* If she could have strangled him with a look alone he would have already fallen to the floor.

'You make me want to be a better person.'

Her throat tightened and her skin crawled.

He stepped towards her and extended his slender fingers towards her face. Something pinched her hard. Her legs gave way as she swooned.

Her throat quivered on the edge of a scream. Head throbbing, she was disorientated, lost, stupid. This was a nightmare, a dream; any moment she would wake up and it would all be over. He carried her, cradling her head and behind her knees. Then she was sinking into a car seat and still her voice failed her.

The car was heading out of the city. Even if her brain had been working properly, they were travelling too fast to risk jumping from the vehicle; perhaps, she thought, she'd escape when they stopped at some traffic lights. Daniel's voice sounded crystal clear through the car speakers. The damned stereo was reciting his poetry.

"What do I have to offer you, but poetry and true love?

An infinite heart that never beats

A face scarred by too many ages

Pages of my life which curl at the corners

Previous bookmarks left by long lost lovers

My cover pristine in a moon light dream that will never end

The clock's hands warp and bend

Coiling into a figure eight fallen on its side

Endless empty rooms of dead potential

Just graves above ground without corpses

Sources of solitude and sorrow

There is no tomorrow

Only the infinity of the moment

and a past always far too present for comfort."

The recording gave his voice an extra layer of something warm and deep. Amalthea found the sound hypnotic and, yawning, she realised how tired she felt and how hot the car was.

"Sweet and sure sanctuary surrounds your soul

Soothing and warm,

shelter from the storm.

Slipping into the perfect circles of your eyes,

I fall head first with only the broken compass of my heart as a guide

I feel you inside

Under pale and worn flesh

Quickening this dead thing

I can hear your soul sing

In a minor key of being free whilst playing with your locks…"

Amalthea woke in a strange bed. The room was oppressively dark. Letting her eyes adjust, she realised that what appeared to be a sliver of sunlight framed two parallel rectangles on the wall opposite her bed. Staring harder, she realised they were shutters and wandered over to open them.

The room filled with light. Beyond the window stretched a large lawn studded with trees and hemmed in by an ancient stone wall. She pushed open the sash and leaned outside. The drop was no more than twelve feet, but there was nothing to use to climb out and a flagstone path waited directly below. If she jumped it was likely she would break a bone or two.

She heard the click of a lock and spun around, feeling inexplicably guilty. The door opened and Daniel stepped into the room. He screwed up his eyes against the brightness of the light.

'You're awake,' he said. 'Would you like breakfast in here or will you join me in the kitchen?'

Amalthea took a step forward. 'Is there coffee?'

'Yes.'

Amalthea followed him into a showroom-style kitchen. Daniel's wealth screamed from every surface, from the flagstone floor to the pristine Aga oven. She had never been so out of place in her life. Watching him carefully, she took of sip from the cup he handed to her.

'We have eggs, bacon, sausages, croissants, jam, cake, fruit and toast. Do you prefer orange, grapefruit or apple juice?' he asked.

'No meat,' she said. 'Anything else is fine. Croissants, jam and orange juice, that sounds good.'

'Coming up.' He served her with a loaded plate and a glass of what appeared to be freshly squeezed juice then he sat opposite her, watching.

'What are you going to eat?' Amalthea stared at him then glanced at her own full plate.

'I woke a couple of hours ago. I already had breakfast.'

'Can I have more coffee please?' she asked, standing up.

'Let me,' he replied, taking her cup to the opposite end of the kitchen where a full coffee jug was being kept warm on an electric hot plate.

He returned with two mugs and passed hers across the table, placing it beside her juice. Her muddled thoughts fell into place, she saw a large window over an old fashioned square sink that was surrounded by empty work surfaces. To the left of the window was a glass paned door that stood slightly ajar. Knowing that she was not locked in made her feel slightly safer, but she had already seen the large garden and the trees beyond its stone outer walls and knew there was not a road or any other house in sight. How isolated was this place? The open door might simply be a ploy so she did not feel trapped.

'Where are we?' she asked.

'In the kitchen… of my home… in Scotland.'

'Where in Scotland?' Amalthea asked.

'A little north of Perth,' he answered.

She nodded. 'How far away is the nearest town or village?'

He shrugged. 'A couple of miles, I guess.'

'Do I get a guided tour of your home?'

'I'll show you around. Have you finished?'

She nodded although four pastries remained, untouched, on her plate.

'Obviously this is the kitchen,' he told her. 'There's a double fridge that I keep well stocked. There's also a wine-rack down here - all reds. Is that okay or shall I get some white wine in for you?'

'Red's fine. What's through there?' she asked as they passed a closed wooden door with a keyhole.

'The pantry.' Daniel kept walking.

She noticed a knife block on the granite work surface and a hook with keys hanging from it by the back door. As she followed Daniel, she scanned every wall for weapons, keys and exit routes. They entered a large room with flocked wallpaper, an imposing leather three piece suite and a dominating fireplace, over which hung an intricately carved sword sheath. She remembered with a sense of doom the origins of the word vagina and shuddered. An ornate handle protruded from the elegant container. It appeared to be an ornamental samurai sword, a katana. Was it sharp?

'The living room,' he said. 'We have lots of books here, a music system and a television set. There are countless channels, but most of them seem pretty pointless, to be honest.'

They crossed the hallway again and Amalthea glanced at the front door. It was probably locked, but there were two windows, one on either side. They entered another room with a table large enough to seat twelve people.

'The dining room,' he said.

She nodded, doubting her ability to keep up the pretence of interest much longer. He was hardly an engaging host. His words were empty and the same hollowness filled the house as if no one actually lived here and it was simply a scene in a movie. She reminded herself that she was searching for weapons and noted a few pictures on the deep red wall, but nothing to wound him. He walked around the table and motioned to a black object on a shelf.

'There's a music system in here too.' He sounded proud as if what he owned was the result of some great and heroic quest.

He passed her again and exited the room. There was a narrow corridor to the right just beyond the mouth of the staircase.

'What's along there?'

'I'll show you,' he said.

It led to a smaller living room. Amalthea imagined it would have served as a drawing room when the house was built, centuries ago. More books lined the walls and a comfortable looking tapestry covered chaise longue waited invitingly beneath a shuttered window. Unless her sense of direction had failed her, this window would open out over the same garden as her bedroom window. The only other item in this room was a large lamp, heavy enough to do some damage.

'That's the toilet and shower room.' He pointed.

He opened the next door and Amalthea glanced inside. The room appeared like most of the bathrooms she had seen. A wooden medicine cabinet was screwed to the only tile-free wall. She stepped inside the room and opened it. There were no medicines, no razors and no toothbrushes inside.

The final door led to a cold room with a stone floor. Empty shelves covered two of the walls and another closed door hung on the final wall. On one top shelf she noticed the edge of a single wooden box.

'I think this was a workshop. The garage is through there,' he said, pointing at the second door.

He didn't open the door and left the room through the one by which they'd entered. He climbed the stairs with Amalthea following. Stained glass windows covered the wall where the stairs veered left and continued their ascension. A few paintings of landscapes hung there and Amalthea realised that she had noticed no photographs or anything that resembled a family portrait.

'This is your room, of course.' Daniel pointed towards a door on the right. 'And this is mine.'

'Can we go in?' Amalthea asked.

'Not just now. It's a bit messy,' he replied.

'This is the bathroom.' He opened the door to a large room with marble tiles on the walls and floors and an elegant footed bathtub. 'You are welcome to consider this your bathroom,' he told her. 'I've got an en suite. I bought you a toothbrush and paste. If you need a different brand let me know. There's also shampoo and conditioner, bubble bath and shower gel. I don't think I forgot anything.'

'Is there a razor… for shaving my legs?'

He looked at her strangely. 'I – I'm sorry. I didn't think… I'll get one for you.'

'I won't be here long. There's no need.'

'Just in case. I want you to have everything you desire while you're here.'

'I guess you'd better get sanitary towels too then.'

He blanched.

He took her to three other doors on that level. 'I haven't done anything in these rooms yet apart from add a bed and wardrobe. Sorry if they seem a bit characterless. I don't use them.'

'What's upstairs?' she asked.

'More empty rooms. This place has twelve bedrooms. Do you want to see?'

'An attic too?'

'Sure,' he said. 'There's another set of stairs up to the attic. It's empty though.'

'Can I see?'

'Of course. Do you want to wander by yourself or shall I come with you?'

'I'm fine by myself.' She climbed the next staircase. The rooms up there were shuttered too; she opened them to let the daylight enter. The rooms were empty, but clean. In some of them second doors led to unused wardrobes and cupboards, but the hiding possibilities were limited, there were no weapons and the windows were far too high to use as a means for escape unless she planned to get out onto the roof. The attic, when she finally reached it, was bare except for a few spider webs. Shadows reached for her in the deathly quiet, empty space and she shivered with cold and fear then quickly left, shutting the door behind her.

~ 8 ~

When she returned, she found a note from Daniel in the kitchen "Popped out for a few minutes. Please help yourself to lunch." She opened the refrigerator then closed it again, wondering how much time she would have. What did Daniel mean when he said "a few minutes"?

She climbed the staircase and tried his bedroom door. It was locked so she hurried back downstairs to the workshop. The second door wasn't locked; it opened easily when she pressed the handle. It led, as he had said it would, into a garage. There was no car inside, but a number of tools on rough pine shelves that might prove useful. She tried opening the external garage door, but that was locked. Shutting the interior doors behind her, she returned to the hallway checked the front then the kitchen door and found both locked. She remembered the keys and looked for them. The larger set had gone, presumably Daniel had taken them with him, but there was a smaller set left. She pulled these off the wall and tried all the locked doors, but none of the keys fitted any of the locks. Frustrated she tried the last door, the door Daniel had told her led to the pantry. It opened with the second key, but instead of shelves laden with food or cooking utensils she saw a narrow wooden staircase leading downwards.

Nervously, she glanced over her shoulder. She heard nothing inside or outside the house and decided to risk descending the stairs. She pocketed the keys and pulled the door shut behind her. She felt her way in the dark until on the fourth step down something brushed her forehead. Clinging to the bannister with one hand, she reached up with the other, found a string and pulled it. Lights flickered on before and above her.

She followed the stairs downwards into a cellar. At the bottom she saw a square room with a metal hoop attached to a wall and a chain arranged in a spiral on the flagstone floor. In one corner of the room was an archway. The hall beyond was lit and she heard something like whispers coming from it. Behind her she heard the sound of a car engine. Daniel must have returned. She stood still for a moment, not knowing whether to investigate further or run back up the stairs and lock the door. Softly, she called out. 'Is anyone there?'

For the briefest of moments everything was silent then Amalthea heard a rush of voices - at least three female voices all talking at the same time, soft and quickly so it was impossible for her to make sense of any of the words. Then she heard one single voice, strong and clear. 'Help us.'

'I can hear Daniel's car. I have to go and lock the door. I'll be back as soon as I can. How many of you are there? Are you locked up?'

'Three, I think. There used to be four. We're chained to the walls. Please hurry. Help us before he comes back.'

'I can't. I don't have time, but I'll be back. I promise.'

'Hopefully before he chains you up too. Don't tell him you know about us. Keep it a secret.'

'Okay.' Amalthea's voice trembled. 'I'm sorry.'

She ran up the stairs, locked the door, remembered that she had left on the light, unlocked the door again and switched the light off. She had locked the door and just replaced the keys on their hook when she heard Daniel's footsteps along the hall from the garage and workshop. She tried to shop shaking, but found it impossible so she picked up his note, pretending to read.

He placed a carrier bag on the counter.

'Can I go out?' Amalthea asked.

He glanced over her shoulder at the window. 'It's pretty cold and damp outside, today.'

'Okay. Can I use your phone?'

'I have to charge it first,' Daniel told her.

Amalthea nodded. 'Okay then. Let me know when it's charged won't you?'

'Of course. Have you had lunch yet?' he asked.

'No.'

'What do you want?'

'Oh, just coffee please,' Amalthea said. Her heart pounded painfully against her ribs.

'You'll waste away.'

Amalthea grimaced at his words.

'Are you okay?' he asked. His face seemed full of genuine concern and she found it impossible to reconcile the display of emotion with the voices downstairs.

Who are you? Instead of asking her question aloud, she sat down and combed her fingers through her hair, trying to stay calm.

'You're safe here,' he assured her.

'And what about my friends, my mum, my job? What about my degree?'

Daniel eyes searched her face. 'Would you like me to

tell them you're okay?'

'How?' She straightened up and put her shaking hands flat against the table top.

'Drive back to Glasgow?'

'Can I come too?' Amalthea asked.

'It's probably safer if you don't,' Daniel replied.

She thought of the women in the basement. Glasgow was probably an hour away and sending Daniel there might have given her time to release the women in the cellar, but what if he took the keys? Then she'd use the tools from the garage or she'd run until she found help. 'Would you mind? Tell them I'm safe. That I'll be back soon.'

'Of course. I'll head over this evening. If you're sure you'll be okay.' His eyes appeared soft and kind, but she knew better than to trust him.

'What day is it?' she asked.

'Thursday, I think.'

'Then there's plenty of shows I can watch on telly. I'll be fine alone for a couple of hours.'

He frowned and Amalthea hoped he didn't suspect anything. He walked across to the coffee pot and she noticed him glance towards the keys hanging beside the back door. She prayed she had replaced them exactly as they were and they weren't moving in a way that suggested they'd been recently touched. He picked up the pot and filled it with water and coffee.

'Tell me about yourself,' Amalthea said as he passed her a mug of steaming black coffee.

His eyes lit up and a huge smile washed over his face. 'Really?'

'Yes. If we're going to be living here together for a while maybe I'll write about you as one of my characters. Would you like that?' she asked.

He nodded.

'Where were you born?'

He sat down at the table. 'In a town called Cirencester. Have you heard of it?'

She shook her head.

'It's a small down in the West of England. Pretty, I guess. They held a big market there every week, still do. I lived on the outskirts, between the town and some woods. It was fun exploring as a boy. I loved to watch birds and animals, especially at night when it was quiet. How about you?'

'Me?' She wasn't expecting the question to be asked in return and felt on edge. *I bet you know all about me.*

'Where were you born?'

She shrugged, dismissively. 'Oh, in Glasgow, on a rather ugly high-rise estate. Do you have any brothers or sisters?'

'I have two half-sisters. We don't really see much of each other though. You?'

'I'm an only child. After my dad left, Mum wasn't really interested in dating. She thought all men were bastards.' Amalthea laughed, nervously.

'I suspect you've inherited a little of that.' Daniel smiled.

Amalthea shrugged. 'Probably.'

'Have you ever had a boyfriend?' he asked.

'Once, about four years ago. It lasted a week. How about you?'

'No boyfriends,' he laughed. 'A fair few girlfriends, but nothing that's really lasted.'

'Are you rich?'

He narrowed his eyes and shifted uncomfortably in his seat. 'Yeah, I guess so, but I've never really thought about it.'

'I'm not. I struggle to get by. I hope I still have my job when I get back though. Speak to my boss, please. I can't afford to lose it.'

'Sure. How long have you been working there?' Daniel asked.

'About a year,' she answered, vaguely.

'I'm sure they won't sack you.'

Amalthea frowned. 'Bar work… it ties in with Uni or College. They'll replace me really quickly if I don't show.'

'I'll make sure I give him a good reason for your short absence,' he promised.

'How short?' Amalthea's tongue flicked out to moisten her lips.

Daniel seemed to relax. 'I guess that depends.'

~ 9 ~

After a light supper of grilled aubergine bake, the left overs of which were enough to feed at least four more people, Amalthea made her excuses and vacated the kitchen, saying she needed a bath. Daniel told her he'd wait until she came back down then head off to Glasgow to speak to her boss and check on her friends. She thanked him.

She put her ear to the bathroom floor, hoping to hear Daniel's movements below, but if he made any sound it must have been muffled by the distance between them. She gave up and ran a bath, pouring scented oil into the water and humming in what she hoped was a natural and relaxed way. She wanted to put him at ease so he wouldn't decide to stay.

When she returned to the kitchen the plates had been washed and the left overs were gone. He checked again that she was comfortable with his leaving. She said yes and headed for the living room to switch on the television.

'You really watch this stuff?' he asked.

'Never miss an episode.' She exhaled audibly and coughed to cover it up then silently cursed herself for her nervousness. 'It's a window into people's lives, like watching people argue in the club.'

He frowned, but didn't ask more. She was relieved. Part of her wanted to blurt out that it was all lies and she was sorry, but she held that part firmly in check. *Go, go, go,* she pleaded silently.

'Okay then.' He checked his watch. 'I imagine it'll take me at least three hours to get everything done, so expect me back at around ten or a bit later. Do you need anything while I'm out?'

'Have we got enough coffee?'

He grinned. 'I'll buy some more, just in case.'

He jangled his keys and left the room, heading towards the garage. She listened for the car engine and within five minutes heard it pull away from the house and get quieter until the sound faded to silence once more. She switched off the television set and checked outside to make certain he had gone. She stood at the window for at least five minutes, terrified he had forgotten something and would return, or that his absence was a trick, a test, and he would walk back up the driveway at any moment. As time ticked away, she balanced the risk of delaying for too long or not long enough and decided just standing there was making her feel sick. She withdrew from the window and left the room.

The keys were no longer on the hook. She tried the

cellar door, but of course it was locked. She hurried to the garage and checked the shelves. There was a crowbar and powerful shears that she hoped might tackle a metal chain. She took a saw as well in case the shears weren't strong or sharp enough for the job. Juggling everything, afraid of dropping something sharp and heavy on her feet, she made her way back to the kitchen.

The gap between door and jam was just wide enough for the tip of the crowbar. She pushed it into the gap and strained against the handle. The door wobbled and a chunk of wood splintered off. Amalthea's heart beat faster. There was no turning back now. She would have to flee when this was done. He'd see the damage the moment he took one step into the kitchen. Hopefully she and the others would be far away by then. Where would they go? She decided not to think about that just yet. *Get the door open first, think about other things later.*

She pushed the crowbar into the gap, which had widened where parts of the wood had broken and fallen away, and forced the handle again. This time there was a satisfyingly loud click and the door swung open towards her. Leaving the crowbar on the top stair she reached for the light pull. She had to take a couple of steps down before she reached it, but was careful not to trip. Cold light illuminated the room and, absolutely terrified, she proceeded, feeling as though she was descending into hell itself, dreading what she might find beyond that wall.

'Hello,' she called out.

'You're back,' a rasping voice replied.

She headed towards the archway, bracing herself for whatever she might find, and entered a smaller room. On a mattress at the far side a naked woman was curled up and appeared to be unconscious, perhaps sleeping. Beside her was a plate full of the same bake she and Daniel had eaten for dinner and a plastic beaker full of red liquid.

'Over here,' the voice called.

Amalthea stepped through another archway into a similarly sized alcove and saw a second woman; this one was sitting up and her green eyes blinked rapidly as if the light hurt them. Around her throat was a metal collar with a chain that was attached to the wall.

'Next room,' the voice summoned Amalthea.

'Just a moment,' she answered and knelt down in front of the woman. The smell hurt her nose and she realised the mattress was probably drenched in urine. This woman had angry sores on her legs and stomach and was dressed in a tiny negligée that was split at the front and revealed almost all of her body. She was desperately thin. Her ash blonde hair was long and tangled and Amalthea wondered how long she had been Daniel's prisoner. Was this what would become of Amalthea if he returned too quickly?

'That's Charlie,' the voice said.

'How long have you been here?' Amalthea asked.

The blonde woman didn't answer.

'She likes music. Switch the radio on.'

Amalthea spotted a small music player. She turned it on and gentle trance music filled the space. It was risky, playing the music and she knew she would not be able to hear if Daniel approached, however the joy on Charlie's face made the risk worthwhile and the emaciated woman seemed to be transported by the sound, away from this dank and filthy dungeon to somewhere beautiful. Amalthea crossed the threshold to yet another room.

In front of Amalthea there stood a pale-skinned, dark-haired beauty, completely naked except for a piece of black cloth that was wrapped around her eyes. Her body was thin, but she appeared stronger than the others.

'Hello, I'm Tay.'

The woman fumbled with the knot in her blindfold.

'Can I help?'

She fiercely shook her head. 'I can do it.'

Finally the delicate fingers succeeded in untying the knot and she removed the cloth from her eyes. 'I'm Moira.' She blinked rapidly, opening and closing her pale blue eyes against the bright light.

Amalthea showed her the wire cutters and handsaw. 'One of these has got to break the chains, right?'

'Are you setting us free?' the woman asked.

'Yes,' Amalthea answered.

'That's what I should have done.' Tears rolled down Moira's face.

Amalthea stepped forward and embraced her. Moira smelled repugnant and trembled violently within Amalthea's grasp, but Amalthea did not pull away for a long time, not until the woman managed to compose herself again.

'May I?' Moira asked, extending a hand towards Amalthea.

Amalthea nodded and passed across the heavy cutters. The sudden weight dragged on Moria's arm, but she recovered herself quickly. She sat on the floor with her legs spread as she lined up the chain in front of her and held it in place under her knees then lifted the middle section a little and placed it within the gaping mouth of the shears. Using both her hands, making her biceps tremble, she pushed the mouth closed and with a loud snap, followed by two clunks, the chain was severed. Moira leapt up and rushed to the next bed to release Charlie.

The three of them continued to the third woman.

'Diane,' Moira said, shaking her arm gently.

The woman's eyes flicked open; they were a strange violet hue that seemed to clash with her mousey-brown hair.

'This is Tay. She's setting us free.'

'Free?' Diane asked. She pushed herself up to a seated position and held the chain out for all to see.

Moira grabbed hold and snapped it as easily as she had broken the others.

'Can you walk?' Moira asked.

Diane stood up. 'I think so.'

Moira faced Amalthea and clasped both her hands. 'Before we leave this place there is something I must do. Will you help us again?'

Amalthea nodded. 'What is it?'

'We have to kill him.'

Amalthea gasped. 'Daniel?'

'Is that going to be a problem for you?' Moira asked.

Amalthea stared into Moira's defiant eyes and felt completely humbled by the power of this captured beauty. 'How?'

'Did you notice any weapons around the place?'

'There's a sword above the fireplace. I don't know if it's sharp,' Amalthea said.

'Okay, we'll test it.' Moira cut the chain again and picked up a five foot segment of it. 'This will keep him at bay for a while. You three can have a chain each. I'm taking the sword.'

'What are you going to do?' Amalthea asked.

'We're going to wait for him to come home and I will sever his head from his body.'

Amalthea gasped. 'Do you think you can?'

'I fucking know I can, Tay. I've never felt so strong in

all my life,' Moira said.

Amalthea considered the two other women. It was obvious they did not share Moira's strength. 'Maybe we should just get them to safety first?'

'They won't be able to walk far. How far are we from the nearest town?'

'A long way, I think,' Amalthea answered.

'We'll need his car.'

'He's taken it with him.'

'When will he be back?' Moira asked.

Amalthea checked her watch. 'Might be as little as an hour, but more likely two.'

'Okay. We'll get washed and I'm afraid we'll need to borrow some clothes.' Moira used a hand flourish to demonstrate her nakedness while Amalthea focused on the woman's face.

Amalthea nodded.

'And we need to figure out the best place to wait for him.'

'The workshop,' Amalthea said.

'Where?' Moira asked, eagerly.

'I'll show you. He needs to go through it to get from the garage to the house. We can wait behind the door.'

'What if he smells us?' Diane asked.

Moira and Amalthea looked at Diane simultaneously as if they had both forgotten they were not completely alone.

'If we get really clean perhaps he won't. Whatever happens though, we need to do this. We need to stop that bastard,' Moira said through gritted teeth. 'If we don't… even if we somehow manage to hide from him for the rest of our lives… there will be more victims. He's sick and he isn't going to stop. Not unless we stop him.'

'I'm afraid,' Diane admitted.

Charlie nodded in agreement.

'Of course you are,' Moira said. Her eyes were soft and gentle but her words were cold and hard. 'I am too.'

'They can wait in my room,' Amalthea suggested.

'So he can find them if we fail?' Moira said. 'This might be our only chance to go home. We should do this together. Refuse to let him frighten you anymore.'

'I know he's a man, but with four against one the odds are absolutely in our favour. He can't be that strong.' Amalthea looked at each woman in turn and exuded the strength she knew they needed to see.

'She doesn't know,' Diane said.

Amalthea looked from Diane to Moira. 'Know what?'

Charlie fell to the floor; the movement was dramatic and yet strangely graceful. She bent her throat and pointed to her jugular vein.

Amalthea shrugged. 'I don't understand.'

'Daniel is a vampire,' Moira told her.

Amalthea laughed then covered her mouth and stood silently. She had no words with which to answer. The three women's faces told her that they believed what they were saying and she imagined how frightened he must have made them, day after day. It was no wonder that they had made the man into a monster in their collective imaginations. He was a monster, albeit not one with supernatural powers.

~ 10 ~

Diane and Charlie slouched on a sofa.

'You two should get washed up,' Moira said as she lifted the ornate sword off two hooks above the fireplace. 'Tay, would you help them get organised?'

Amalthea nodded, although really she wanted to watch Moira handle the katana. Moira stroked the enamelled sheath with her left hand as she held the handle in her right then she grasped it and slid it off. The steel glinted cruelly. It certainly appeared sharp enough.

'Please, Tay, we need you.'

The plea broke beyond Amalthea's reverie and she guided one woman in each of her arms towards the upstairs bathroom. She ran a warm, but not too hot bath then automatically reached for a bottle of oil, but quickly decided against pouring it into the water. Even a pleasant smell might have given them away. Diane was already stripped naked so she helped Charlie out of her negligee and supported each woman as they climbed into the bath. Their hair was filthy and tangled and Amalthea washed it for them. Both the women looked much better without the grime. She glimpsed beyond their emaciation and saw their former beauty. She pulled a towel from the heated rail, helped Diane step out of the bath and wrapped her in its warm fibres then she did the same for Charlie.

'Dry yourselves,' she told them. 'I'll be back in a moment.'

She headed out of the bathroom, rushed down the stairs and came face to face with Moira who was standing, sword in hand, with a wide grin on her face.

'It's sharp.' Moira pointed at a chair in the far corner of the room or more accurately an ex-chair that had been sliced into two. One half leaned against a wall and the other rocked on its jagged side on the floor.

'Wow!' Amalthea nodded.

'I'd better get cleaned up as well. Can we all borrow clothes please?'

'Of course. Follow me.'

Amalthea jogged up the stairs as Moira followed behind with the unsheathed sword still in her hand.

'Be careful with that,' Amalthea said.

'Uhh, oh yeah.' Moira chuckled.

Amalthea sat, patiently, at the top of the stairs for the unlikely warriors to return, unable to stop her body from shaking and terrified of what was to come. Amalthea wasn't even sure she wanted Daniel to die. Perhaps he was a monster, but surely running away and letting the authorities deal with him was the only solution that made sense in a civilised world, certainly not slicing someone into pieces. There were too many things that could go wrong with Moira's plan. What if they froze at the sight of Daniel, unable strike the fatal blow? What would he do then? She stared at the bathroom door, trying to find words to convince Moira of the folly of her plan. *What if it were me, chained up in the basement? Would I want to kill him?* She didn't think she could take that away from Moira as well? At least this way the women would have closure of one kind or another.

The three women stepped out from the bathroom. Amalthea's clothes fit them poorly, but even so it was wonderful to see them looking… human. No longer chained animals or slaves, but people who were able to make their own choices, their own mistakes. Amalthea's fear subsided as she realised she wasn't responsible for them. They hadn't had any choices for far too long and it was time to let them make their own decisions. If that meant they killed Daniel, so be it. She would not stand in their way and, if she was needed, she would help them. Moira held the sword confidently and the smile on her face was beautiful and calm, empowered.

'Show us this workshop, please Tay,' Moira said.

'Is this what you all want to do?' Amalthea asked.

All three nodded.

'It's what we have to do,' Moira answered.

Amalthea stood up and led the way.

Moira checked the door to the garage and found that it opened towards them into the workshop, creating a blind spot behind it that would fit one person easily, two at a squeeze.

She peered into the garage. Amalthea flicked on the light for her and a bright fluorescent strip blinked into life.

'Nowhere in there. I guess we'll all have to wait in here. So how are we going to do this? The door will open and block this area from Daniel's vision. Diane and Charlie do you want to stand behind there with the chains? I can wait on the other side. If he sees me before I get chance to swing I'll need you to restrain him as best you can with those chains, okay?'

'Where do you want me?' Amalthea asked.

Moira smiled in a way that sent shivers of anticipation along Amalthea's spine. 'How about in that corner?' She pointed at the far left wall, facing the garage door. 'Do you want a chain or the crowbar?'

'Crowbar,' Amalthea answered.

'Good choice.' Moira winked. 'A girl after my own heart.'

Amalthea blushed. Like a teenager crushing on an older girl at school, she was as much in love with her poise and commanding personality as she was with her beauty. She desperately hoped that, when all this was over, she'd have the chance to get to know Moira better.

'Light on or light off?' Amalthea asked.

'Off,' the three said together.

'But will we be able to see well enough to attack?' Amalthea asked.

'We've been living in a dark cellar for months. We can see in the dark. Plus chances are the garage will be lit. Did you switch the light off in there?'

'I'll check.' Amalthea opened the garage door and switched off the light.

'Ready?' Moira asked.

The women got into position and Moira extinguished the light. On a tiny sliver of illumination, from the hallway beyond, remained.

'Maybe we should sit while we wait?' Amalthea said.

'Don't fall asleep,' Moira warned.

'I don't think we'll have time. Unless I'm mistaken, isn't that the sound of a car engine?' Amalthea whispered.

'I can hear it too,' Moira said. 'Okay, stand up, it's show time.'

~ 11 ~

The garage door chugged upwards and the clanking of chains made the room feel colder. Amalthea imagined the others were shivering with dread too – he had returned. *What now?* She opened her mouth to whisper "wait", to renegotiate on Daniel's behalf, or was it on her behalf, she wasn't sure. She swallowed the word. He didn't deserve their mercy. *Chaining Moira for all those months, years… How dare one imprison such a wild spirit?* It was unforgivable and Amalthea would not plead for his life, but what if they failed? What if he scared them all so deeply that the women crumpled and folded as he stepped into the room? Would it be up to Amalthea to finish what Moira started? She didn't know whether she could. Again the word "wait" rose to her throat like a hiccup, but at that moment the car engine was switched off and the rooms descended into a silence that was broken only by the squeak of a car door opening and the sound of suction as it was pushed closed, the tapping of footsteps and the churning and clunking of chains as the garage door descended. There was no light beyond the door. Daniel did what he needed to do in the dark and Amalthea suddenly realised that he would see them the moment he stepped into the room. Her fear rose to a new precipice and she smelled panic around her as the same realisation dawned on the others, but it was too late to run. Amalthea raised the crowbar and made ready to strike… strike then run… if she knocked him out at least, they might still get away alive.

She heard the door handle click then silence returned. She imagined him waiting on the other side of that narrow wood barrier, knowing their exact positions in the workshop. He knew they were waiting in the dark for his return and that Amalthea had betrayed him, rescuing and releasing the women he had chained in the dark. She sensed his anger and bitter disappointment as he paced around the garage, deciding what to do. She checked her imagination and realised it was creating his actions; he wasn't pacing the length of the garage; there was no sound of footsteps. For some reason, that Amalthea was unable to fathom, he must have been standing perfectly still behind the door. What was he waiting for?

Time crawled as if someone pressed a button marked slow motion. Every breath Amalthea took seemed to last an hour, and she focused on the progression of air into and out of her lungs millimetre by agonising millimetre. The time between exhaling and inhaling made her panic as if she would run out of air and die. The taunting cruelty of her own imagination caused her to visualise the fine hairs on Daniel's hand, in the darkness, beyond the physical barrier of the door, and she watched a bead of sweat blossom and roll down his brow. He didn't move his hand to wipe it away and his fingers lingered, motionless, less than an inch from the door handle, caught in a bubble of time that seemed as though it would last an eternity then the door clicked and time sped up. Before Amalthea realised what was happening Daniel stood in the workshop surrounded by the three women. She watched helplessly as Diane and Charlie wrapped chains around his wrists. He shook his right arm and Diane flew against a wall and bounced off it onto the floor. Moira held the sword in two hands behind her shoulder and swung. He ducked and it whistled through the air above his head. Taking a step back, Moira reversed the sword and swung again.

'Daniel,' Amalthea said.

He faced her. Tears rolled down his cheeks and his eyes pleaded for an answer to one question. "Why?"

'You can't make prisoners out of people,' Amalthea said, although she wasn't entirely sure whether she made any noise at all; perhaps she just thought the answer.

'I only wanted…'

With an elegant yet ruthless swing, the sword hit Daniel's neck on its second arc and cut into his spinal cord. Moira tugged it away from the bone and muscle as the other women made stifled gagging sounds. Daniel's head hung at an odd angle, but he kept speaking. 'To be…'

A slash from the opposite side hacked into his throat.

The skin flapped open and the muscle beneath created a grotesque necklace.

'Loved.'

With a final, full-body swing, so powerful it made Moira stagger and lose her footing, Daniel's head was severed. It flew through the air towards Amalthea, landing dramatically at her feet. His eyes stared up at her. The bloodless, bodyless head stared into her eyes, mouth still moving and softly dimpled cheeks still twitching. Amalthea had fallen down the rabbit hole; it wasn't happening. It wasn't real. *Wake up!*

'I'm sorry.' His last words were spoken and his face was no longer animated; Amalthea released the scream she had imprisoned and the sound echoed around the workshop. The other women covered their ears to protect themselves from the relentlessly slicing sound.

She sensed a presence beside her and two shaking arms were wrapped around her upper body. She stopped screaming.

'It's time to go,' Moira told her.

'What just happened?' Amalthea asked trying to drag air into her empty lungs.

'He's dead,' Moira answered. 'Let's go.'

Amalthea shook her head, but Moira clasped her hand and pulled her towards the garage. As they passed Daniel's headless body, Charlie knelt beside it searching his pockets.

She pulled out and jangled a set of keys.

'Should we bury him?' Diane asked.

'I just want to go home,' Moira said.

Amalthea heard the conversation and tried to nod, but she felt as distant as a star in the night sky and completely unable to communicate.

'We'll go to Glasgow first. Hopefully we can get some sense out of her when we hit the city.'

Moira pushed Amalthea into the front passenger seat and strapped a seat belt around her torso. Diane and Charlie got into the back as Moira fired up the engine and switched on the lights. 'Dammit. The doors.'

'I'll get them,' Charlie said, bounding excitedly out of the car like a puppy on its first walk.

Amalthea stared blankly as the metal door shunted upwards. Moira drove beneath it to their freedom.

'There was no blood,' Amalthea whispered.

'Welcome back, Tay. I thought we lost you back there. What did you say?' Moira asked.

They were still in the car. Amalthea peered at the other two cuddled and asleep on the back seat. Moira seemed alert and comfortable driving.

'No blood,' Amalthea repeated, finding her voice.

'I guess that's what happens with vampires.' Moira shrugged.

'Vampires don't exist,' Amalthea said.

'Then you explain why his neck didn't bleed when we chopped off his head?'

'I can't.'

'Vampire,' Moira said, firmly.

Amalthea nodded. She had no better answer. 'How did you know?'

'That he wasn't human?'

'Yes.'

'A thousand little things and a few larger ones: he barely touched any food and when he did it seemed like he was just trying to appear normal. He stank of blood, frequently and I saw dried remains of it in the crease of his mouth once or twice. He even told me when I asked. I was chained up by then, of course, but I knew he was telling me the truth at last,' Moira said.

'I didn't know. I thought you were just scared of him.' Hot tears formed in Amalthea's eyes.

'Vampires exist.'

'You don't think he's the only one?' Amalthea asked.

'He may be a freak, but he never struck me as something marvellously unique.'

~ 12 ~

'What about a world trip?' Amalthea asked, resting her head on Moira's shoulder.

Five months had passed. Amalthea had been busy. And now she was living in the tiny Camden bedsit with the love of her life. Writing about vampires, researching them, had become an obsession, but she had no idea what was true and what was fiction.

'The writing might make you a target.' Moira squeezed Amalthea's hand and kissed her fingers.

'Babes, we're already targets. We killed one of them. You think I should stop?'

Moira shrugged then shook her head, stopped and shrugged again. 'I don't know. Sometimes I get scared. It feels like we're being watched.'

Amalthea glanced involuntarily at the window with its closed blind and drawn curtains – belt and braces. 'If they thought we were a threat they'd have already dealt with us.'

'I guess so. I just don't want to lose you. I don't think being so open about what we're doing is the way to go.'

'But it's how we found Robert,' Amalthea said.

'Robert's crazy,' Moira replied.

Amalthea sighed.

'You want danger?' Moira asked.

'I don't know. I want something I can sink my teeth into if you'll excuse the pun.'

Moira grinned and stroked Amalthea's wrist. 'You can sink your teeth into me.'

'Mmmmm.' Amalthea nibbled Moira's throat.

Moira arched her neck and exposed her fluttering pulse for further oral investigation. They kissed and the world spun around them. Hands explored each other's bodies.

Moira pushed Amalthea off her body. 'I just wonder…'

'What?'

Moira stared hard into Amalthea's eyes. 'Whether we're better off letting it go.'

'Always wondering who's waiting round the next corner?' Amalthea asked.

'You sound paranoid,' Moira said.

'Daniel can't be the only one. You said it yourself. There might be hundreds of vampires out there. We don't know. We'll probably never know.'

Moira glanced up at the two katana swords that hung on their apartment wall, more than a simple decoration. 'I wonder what they are?'

'Vampires?'

'Yes. Did Stoker get it right? Are they cursed or are they something else? A genetic mutation or a different species?' Moira pondered.

Amalthea tucked a stray hair behind her ear. 'Does it matter?'

Moira nodded. 'I think so. Know your enemy.'

'Understand your characters.'

'So, what do you want to do this evening? Are we gonna fuck or what?' Moira asked.

Amalthea kissed Moira's hand. 'Yes.'

The Salon of Lost Souls

Laura drove her mini along the gravel drive toward the Stately House that would be her home for the next few years. Yellow stone fascias sparkled where the soft Northern sunlight caressed them. Her nervous excitement subsided a little and, for one blissful moment, it was as though she was being welcomed home.

No other cars littered the driveway. She had passed the visitors' car park a few minutes ago, and she considered driving back there, but decided against it. The removal van would be here soon. When car and van had been emptied she would ask her line manager where she should park overnight.

She stepped out of the car, pushed the door shut and stretched her neck to take in the true height of the building. Corinthian pillars adorned the front, and white sash windows reached skyward above the horseshoe-shaped stone stairs that led to a pair of French doors on the first floor. She let her imagination take flight and saw a grand, horse-drawn carriage empty its contents of proud figures, draped in silks and velvets. The vintage nobility swept up the stairs to be welcomed by the Earl and Countess.

Instead of following their ghostly footsteps, Laura crossed the gravel driveway and entered via the shop in the bowels of the building.

A woman in a green tartan vest was chatting to a grey-haired, camel-coated customer about the selection of single malts. Laura waited patiently. Her eyes flitting from flagstone floor to dark wood desk and across an array of tastefully arranged merchandise. The stock was familiar. They had mostly the same items for sale in Laura's previous workplace. She had counted stock and marked off delivery sheets numerous times and could name both the suppliers and their contact telephone numbers by heart. It wouldn't be so different here after all. Same work, different location. Only this time she was the custodian, the key holder, the resident manager. It was her time. A promotion that seemed almost too good to be true.

The customer wandered thoughtfully away from the sales desk and Laura approached with a warm, professional smile.

'Hi, I'm Laura McIntyre. I'm the new manager. Has Peter Ingles arrived yet?'

The shop assistant returned a confident smile. One that said its owner knew everything there was to know about Laura already. 'He phoned to say he'll be about thirty minutes. I'll call Mike, the deputy manager.'

Laura nodded. She read the name on the staff badge. 'Thank you, Angela. Have you worked here long?'

Angela's smile didn't falter. 'I've been here since the

beginning. Almost twenty five years now. Twenty five years and fifteen managers.'

Laura frowned. Angela's fixed smile was like a knife, gouging a hole in her chest. The feeling of being welcomed home fled under the scrutiny of the older woman's eyes.

'That's a lot of managers.'

'They never stay long. They either quit or die.'

A man in a tweed jacket hurried towards them.

'This is Mike. Mike this is Laura ...'

'Laura McIntyre,' Laura said holding out her hand.

The small man blushed a little and paused before reaching out his hand to shake hers. 'Welcome to Regency Heights, Miss McIntyre. It's good to meet you at last.'

Laura pressed her spine against the back of a forest-green leather armchair. A book rested open on her lap and she sipped a cooling cup of herbal tea. Her head was spinning and she just wanted to relax, but everything was too new, too alien and she couldn't settle.

She thought back over the events of the day, her first day at Regency Heights. Mike had been pleasant, if a little nervous. She understood now why Peter hadn't seen fit to promote him to the manager's position. Although it was still difficult to believe that he trusted her enough, just twenty-eight years old and five years with the organisation, to take care of such a jewel in the crown of the Trust's properties.

But, believable or not, she was here. Her first night as resident manager, surrounded by boxes containing her imported life.

Perhaps it was pure nepotism. The McIntyre and Ingles families were old friends and she and Peter had gone hunting and riding together in years past. Thankfully no one had openly questioned her lack of experience. She guessed her face fit, and she was good at her job. Her calm, organisational skills would be useful. Experienced staff and an unassertive deputy manager were not a great mix when the organisation had plans to improve productivity and streamline staff numbers on the site. Peter assured her that her strength and understanding of the business side of the Trust would be of great value in her new role.

So she had spent her first day meeting the staff, exploring the house, and learning about the alarm systems and local emergency numbers. The staff seemed more interested in what lay behind the locked door of her apartment than in Laura's management style. They had never seen the rooms which she now occupied, and she wouldn't be the first manager to show them. In her job, becoming friends with staff was not advisable. Distance instilled respect and, as many of the stewards were twice her age, she needed all the respect she could command. Angela's aloofness still intimidated her a little. It was almost as though the shop assistant didn't expect Laura to stay for long. Of course that was understandable in the circumstances, but Laura would prove the assumption wrong and show Peter what a capable manager she was. If she turned this place around her career would soar.

Still, the creaking of the old, empty building unnerved her. Echoes of footsteps paced the floor above. Laura knew she wouldn't be able to settle until she had one last check, just to make sure she was alone.

She stepped out, torch in hand, onto the landing of a staircase that reminded her of Escher's Convex and Concave lithograph. The house hummed as if frightened of its own silence. She turned right and stepped into the blue and red veined belly of Regency Heights. The weak glow of her torch beam was swallowed by dark wood. Shadows lurked under furniture and behind paintings. Beyond the grand staircase, huge windows, the only ones that remained unshuttered for the night, loomed, and beyond them trees shook claw-fisted branches threateningly.

Proud, pale faces glared down from the walls at jaded trims of intricate geometry while drill bit decorations covered in gilt, surrounded the closed doors of the State rooms.

Staring at the windows and portraits gave her a sense of vertigo. She was a mouse among ravenous cats. Only the thought of her shotgun and the heavy bolts on the other side of her apartment door gave her the confidence to continue. It was just an old house, an empty old house, an empty, dark and very noisy old house, far away from town, alone among the trees and memories. A movement of green, caught in the corner of her left eye, sent her running back to her apartment. She bolted the door before taking another breath and decided further exploring could wait until daylight. For now a broken night on a soft bed awaited.

Laura rubbed her tired eyes and switched on the coffee maker. The smell of Java brewing warmed the room and made it feel almost homely. Sleep in a new place was always hard to come by. It might take a few restless nights, but soon she would settle into the new routine. Her fears of the previous night seemed ridiculous to her now. The thuds she had taken for footsteps would have been old water pipes, expanding and contracting, and the tuneless humming only the humidifiers, which preserved the priceless oil paintings. She forced a laugh meant to deride her folly. She could invent ghost stories if she wanted, but she wasn't going to be afraid of her own shadow each night after the house had emptied of staff. She was a McIntyre and nothing frightened a McIntyre.

She checked her watch again. It was only six-fifteen and the head steward wouldn't arrive for at least two hours. She peered out of a window and watched a community of birds still sleeping in the branches of the giant horse chestnut. They had the right idea, but returning to bed would be pointless. Coffee, that was what she needed, and the filter machine had already finished brewing her first pot of the day.

That day and the others that followed were easier than Laura expected. The staff seemed to respond well to her firm but fair management style and even Angela's demeanour seemed to soften with time. Only the nights were hard.

At first Laura spent the evenings working in her office, but the footsteps seemed louder there and she sometimes heard the soft chuckles of a child.

Within a week of trembling under the fluorescent strip light, trying to concentrate on the computer screen, she changed her routine and retired to her apartment as soon as she bolted the door behind the last member of staff to leave. Playing music helped, but she couldn't play it loud enough to make the walls tremble for fear of tripping the alarms and she still heard the ticking of the drawing room clock, or the creaking of floorboards, or the whisper of satin, during the gaps between songs.

In daylight hours she would dismiss the silly ghost stories she heard from regular visitors and staff alike – the green lady who glided along hallways and the small child who played hide and seek on the back stairs. But alone at night she imagined the pair of phantoms plotting to tempt her out of her rooms. She woke at five each morning drenched in sweat.

When Laura thought back to her first day and what Angela had said about the house's managers, that they always quit or died, her mind would curl inwards on dark thoughts and wonder how they died and whether those who quit left with their sanity intact. In the day time though, she had it all under control, so it surprised her when Peter remarked with some concern that she wasn't looking at all well.

'I'm fine,' she replied, frowning.

'Are you sure? You're very pale and your eyes look tired.'

'Since when does a boss want someone to be ill?' That sounded a little defensive to her ears so Laura added a self-conscious giggle at the end.

'Why don't you come out to dinner with me this evening? We can get some decent meat into you.'

Laura blushed.

'You know what I mean.'

Was Peter's laugh self-conscious too?

'Sure,' Laura replied. 'It would be good to get out for a few hours.'

'You know being first on call doesn't mean you can't leave the house, don't you?'

Laura shrugged. 'What can I say? It's a nice

apartment.'

The pub was busy, but Peter and Laura found an empty table. The legs wobbled a little and they had to drink the tops off their pints before they could rest safely without fear of spillage. A roaring fire dominated the end of the narrow room and wood smoke filled Laura's nostrils.

'They do a great steak and kidney pie here,' Peter said. 'My treat.'

'I remember the venison pies your mother used to make.' Her stomach rumbled and she realised that the sandwiches and coffee she'd been living off for the past two weeks just wasn't enough. 'I guess I'm hungry.'

'We'll sort that out and you can tell me why you aren't sleeping.'

'What?'

'Oh come on, Laura. We know each other well enough. Something's wrong. Is it the job? You are young. Maybe too young?'

'No, I'm fine. The house is just a bit noisy at night, that's all. I'll get used to it.'

'Are you sure? I don't want to risk the wrath of your father if it makes you ill.'

'It's a great job, a wonderful opportunity. Honestly, I'm grateful.'

'Okay then. Drink up. I'll order the pies and another couple of pints.'

'Watch out, Peter. You're driving.'

'I drive better with a couple inside me.'

Laura shook her head, but didn't bother to argue. Peter was stubborn too.

Laura waved at the Mercedes' rear lights as Peter drove away. Regretting her choice of footwear, she stumbled toward the door. Her bag had become quantum storage space and it took a lot of shaking and rummaging before she found the keys.

'Don't forget the alarm,' she reminded herself, under her breath. She closed her eyes to recall the code number and almost lost her balance. 'Shit! I should not have had that last pint.'

But she did feel pleasantly full and cheerfully drunk. It had been exactly what she needed. A night away from the cold dark house in front of a warm fire with bright company. Peter had offered to see her inside, but she didn't want to risk asking him up to her apartment. They'd always managed to keep on the right side of friendship, but she was undeniably attracted to him, and the house made her lonely. No, it was good he had gone, and now that the keys were in her hand and the alarm code in her head it was time to go to her bed, alone.

The stairs swam as she mounted them. The house called out with all its usual noises. Laura concentrated on clinging to the bannister and putting one foot in front of the other. When she reached the top she realised she didn't remember whether she had locked the door or switched the alarm back on. Knowing she would not descend the stone steps without tumbling down them, she hoped for the best and stabbed at the apartment door with her key until finding the lock and opening it.

Without undressing, Laura collapsed on her bed and slept solidly until her alarm woke her at seven.

After three pints of water and two pots of coffee, Laura's headache faded enough for her to face the day. A natural workaholic, Laura hadn't taken a day off since she'd arrived in the house. However, the thought of sitting in front of a flickering screen and inviting the hangover's return was enough to motivate her to grab some R&R. Eyes shaded by designer sunglasses, she headed outside to explore the woods.

The path was delightfully cool and her gentle stroll took her further and further from the oppressive house and all responsibilities. Her mobile was tucked in her pocket, a safety blanket, just in case she was needed, but it hadn't vibrated so far. Bird song and the chatter of insects were the only sounds here. Not even a jogger or dog walker disturbed the tranquillity. It wasn't until Laura checked her watch that she realised she'd been walking for two hours. Time to head back.

There was a fork in the path that she hadn't noticed from the other direction. There were no signposts or any landmarks to tell her whether she should go left or right. Chances were both paths would eventually lead back to the house, so she took the right fork without letting worry spoil the wonderful day.

A low fence ran parallel to the path. Beyond it she saw gravestones. She definitely had not passed this place before. She clambered over the fence to take a peek. The graves seemed too modest to belong to the family who had owned Regency Heights and most of the inscriptions had worn away with time. Only one grave, among the fifty or more, had been recently tended. Fresh flowers had been placed there, by a descendent Laura assumed. There was no card, but the inscription on the stone marker, while faint, was still visible. Maggie McIntyre, 1824 – 1856, Falsely Accused, Rest in Peace. Laura's skin crawled and she shivered. Now she knew what "someone walked over my grave" felt like.

There was no one in the tiny cemetery, but Laura sensed she was being carefully watched. Her peace was shattered and she felt strangely afraid. She hurried back over the fence and along the path until she reached the fork once more. This time she took the other route back.

Mike was behind the shop counter when Laura returned to

the house.

'Good afternoon,' Mike said with an expression that requested an explanation.

'Any problems?' Laura asked.

'Not at all. So you do take days off sometimes. I was beginning to wonder.'

'I had a lovely walk in the woods. Do you know anything about the graveyard?'

'Graveyard?' Mike asked. 'No. Is it in the woods? The family have a mausoleum at St Anne's. Was it for their pets?'

'I don't think so. Never mind.'

'What are your plans for the rest of your day off?'

'Lunch in the café then a trip to the supermarket I think. Do we need anything for the staffroom?'

'Liz deals with all that, so you can bet they've got everything they need.'

'Have we been busy?'

Mike checked visitor numbers on the till. 'About fifty so far, but the afternoons tend to be busier.'

Laura nodded. 'Well I'll see you later?'

'Okay,' Mike said.

Laura grabbed plenty of cold beef and salad from the supermarket. She also stocked up on coffee, wine and a bottle of vodka to warm her throat and settle her nerves if she needed it. She unpacked all this into her galley kitchen. The pristine but intimidatingly complicated oven remained silently smug as if it was used to being left untouched by the flat's residents. 'One day,' Laura threatened, although she wasn't sure she would ever use it.

She forced herself to avoid work and curled up on the sofa with a book she'd wanted to read for a while. The monotonal hum of the house became a lullaby and before she reached the second chapter Laura was fast asleep.

It was eleven when she awoke. The dark skies oppressed her and she blocked them out with shutters. It was too late for coffee, but vodka might help her return to sleep and she poured herself a generous glass. The house made its usual cracking and humming noises as she sipped the warming liquid and tried to relax. Television would help. She reached for the remote, but froze as a loud shout splintered the air.

'Maggie!'

Someone was in the house.

She grabbed her jacket and pulled out her mobile. No signal, not even for emergency calls. She would have to phone from the land line in the office, but she wouldn't leave her flat unarmed. Cradling the shotgun, she quietly unlocked the door. Glancing to her right she saw the impossible. A beautiful dark haired woman in a long green dress. The woman didn't seem to notice her. She was crossing the landing toward the salon. Without opening the door, she was gone.

Laura shook her head. She was tired. Perhaps she drank the vodka too quickly. Her eyes were playing tricks on her. She would feel foolish if she called the police, only to have imagined the intrusion. She might seem unstable, untrustworthy. Trying not to over think, Laura walked towards the salon door and turned the handle.

Two women faced each other at the centre of the room. The woman in green and another in a silver silk gown whose gloved hands clutched a raised pistol. Between them and the shuttered windows lay a man, surrounded by a deep red stain.

'Whore!' the woman in silver hissed as she aimed at the other woman's face.

'No!' Laura cried.

Ignoring the house manager, the women stood still. The trace of a smile made the woman in green's cheeks twitch. 'I never touched him, Ma'am.' Laura was sure that title had never been uttered in a less respectful and more challenging way. The name Maggie rushed into her head, was that the name of the woman in green?

The countess, if that was who the woman in silver had been, tried to control her shaking arms. She appeared terrified as if it wasn't her who was pointing the gun away from Maggie's face and toward her own.

Laura screamed and lifted her shotgun, not knowing who to aim for or what good it would do. With an eardrum shattering bang both women and the man vanished and Laura fell to the floor, cradling her weapon like a beloved teddy bear while tears streamed down her face.

Laura was drunk by the time the chief steward arrived at eight-thirty. She listened to him move around the house, opening shutters, totally undisturbed by any spectral manifestations. She searched her mind for a believable lie that would save the humiliation of being found this way by her staff. She couldn't take another day off, but the house wouldn't open for a couple of hours. Coffee was the answer and she would drink it until she was at least part way sober.

Everything seemed terribly loud, from the voices of stewards to the roar of the vacuum cleaner as the house was made ready for the public. Laura hid for as long as she was able, venturing out at ten for the staff meeting. Her pep talk didn't seem to inspire the staff who stared at her confused. She wished them a busy day before retreating to her office, glad that the assistant manager had the day off and she would be alone.

She searched through folders and guide books for details of the house's history hoping to clarify or preferably dispel the visions of the previous night. She found nothing about a shooting and as the day wore on she became convinced that it had been a vivid dream, brought on by drinking too heavily. The name Maggie, that was the name she had seen on the grave. No wonder it had entered her dreams. How silly she was to have thought it real. The house would not drive her insane. This was her career and she cared too much about it to be frightened by ghost stories. Logic and pragmatism won out and by the time the shutters were being closed again at the end of the day Laura felt much stronger.

Nothing disturbed her sleep that night or the next. Her belief that it had only been a dream strengthened, and the confrontation in the salon became a distant memory within a week. On her next day off Laura avoided the woods and instead visited town. It stank of fish from the harbour and the locals kept their distance from the well-dressed stranger. Their faces were homogeneous in a way that only small rural towns can maintain. The shops had nothing that interested her and the coffee she drank in the café wasn't as good as the stuff she made with her machine. She was lonely. Far from those she loved. She wanted to go home. Not to Regency Heights but to her real home, where people loved her. To compensate she bought a bottle of vodka from the supermarket before returning to her apartment. How long would she need to prove herself here before she could transfer? It had been less than a month. She might be trapped here for years as her social life imploded. The only way forward was to work hard, and apply for every suitable job that came up. She wouldn't tell Peter how she felt. It would seem ungrateful.

The vodka helped her feel less homesick although the words in her book juddered after the fourth glass. Not wanting to fall asleep too early and risk waking before morning, she switched on the television and watched a documentary about gang war in Brooklyn.

The show helped put things in perspective. She lived a comfortable, even privileged life. She had a lovely apartment in an amazing building, plenty of money and a family who would help her whenever she asked. Sacrificing her social life for a year or two was nothing compared to how some people struggled every day. With a lot of effort she might even befriend some locals and spend evenings in the pub rather than drinking alone. Wrapped in a blurry sense of contentment, Laura eventually fell asleep.

At first she thought the explosive noise had been on the television, but when she opened her eyes the set had powered down and was on standby. Her second thought was the ghostly altercation in the salon. The fiction that it had been simply a dream fled as she stared at her apartment door, listening intently. She might have been sitting that way for one or twenty minutes by the time she heard the gentle knock on her door.

Shit! 'Who is it?'

No reply of course. That would be too sane, too easy. They wanted her outside the locked room. They? Who were they and what did they want with her?

In spite of her conviction she called again. 'Is anyone there?'

Another three raps on the door. *Fuck!*

'I'm calling the police,' she shouted and grabbed her phone. No signal again. She needed to find a more reliable provider.

'I've got a gun.'

A childlike giggle and the patter of feet ran from the door.

Laura figured she had two choices – check outside or go quietly mad inside. Neither seemed an attractive option. Again she remembered Angela's warning that first day. "Twenty five years and fifteen managers. They never stay long. They either quit or die." Could fifteen managers have gone mad? It seemed unlikely. It seemed unlikely that she was mad too. Something or someone was out there and it wanted to drive her screaming from the house. The McIntyre pride she usually relied upon in times of stress shrank away, begging her not to investigate, not this time.

She pulled the covers over her head. The ridiculousness of this "protection" wasn't lost on her. The gun waited in the corner of the room. Would it offer more than a duvet? She scurried on all fours to collect it and returned to her bed and the shelter of her covers. Her heart raced. She wasn't getting any air. The dark room with its locked windows was crushing her. She knew that if she didn't get out of the house she'd suffocate.

The lock clicked. Her fingers hovered over the handle as she strained her ears for sounds beyond the usual humming of the house. A house afraid of its own silence and thus never silent. However, she was afraid of making any noise and alerting anyone's notice. The humming served both their purposes this evening. She opened the door. The door to the salon was wide open and a sickly light spilled out into the hallway. She repositioned her gun and held the barrel before her, taking one silent step toward the room. The light went out and she was surrounded by darkness. Behind the walls she heard a faint scratching noise as if from an animal. Trapped vermin was the least of her worries. It would be a relief to know she shared the house with rats instead of ghosts. But rats wouldn't explain the light, the strange unearthly light that had been extinguished on her approach. *Fuck it!* They knew she was here. She might as well go and see what they were up to in the salon.

Green light surrounded her as Laura stepped tentatively over the threshold. It was brighter than before. It blinded her. She blinked to try and recover her vision. To her right she saw movement, low to the ground. She strode into the centre of the room and scanned the area for anything different. Shadows lost their contrast in this light and it was hard to make sense of anything, but over there, beside the door, something was moving. Something big.

One of the house's treasures was a beautiful but fragile Chippendale sofa. The movement was coming from there. Was something on, under or behind the chair? The shotgun was aimed, but she wouldn't shoot unless she had to. The chair was worth millions. She could never pay for such damage. She would be ruined.

The sofa was deep pink, perhaps it had once been red, but it had taken on an unpleasant brown shade in the strange light. Its gilt legs seemed to be pawing at the floor and the decorative spirals at either end of the back rest were somehow unfurling. Gold tentacles thrashed through the air, reaching for her. Before she had time to reconsider, she fired and woollen fibres exploded from the cushion. Now it charged towards her, wounded and angry. She backed away towards the shuttered windows, clawing at the bolts, trying to make an escape route, even though she knew the fall would kill her. "They either quit or die." Well her resignation was buried in that priceless velvet sofa cushion, would she die too?

A tentacle caught her cheek and ripped skin from muscle. It didn't feel like gilded wood. It didn't feel like anything she recognised. It was dry, but cool, firm but not hard. The wound throbbed with an intense heat. She shot the other barrel and hit the back rest. A hole, almost a foot across allowed Laura to see the door, now closed again. A vortex of green and red light pulsed from the wounded sofa toward her, tugging at her hair and clothes. She would die. She would be sucked into this wormhole in the haunted salon and never be seen again. Or she would be pulled inside out by the pressure and be found in the morning, a bloody mound of flesh. She threw the gun at the sofa in desperate hope.

A loud voice, female and commanding said. 'Not her. She isn't the one.'

As the sofa scurried back to the wall, the vortex spluttered and died. Unable to hold herself upright Laura fell into strong pale arms wrapped in green cotton sleeves.

'It's all right, Miss. You can stand up.'

Laura tested her legs and found the woman was telling the truth. 'What was that?'

'A gateway.'

'To where?'

'Somewhere you do not want to go, Miss.'

Laura stared at the freckled face. 'You saved me.'

'I couldn't let my own blood get sucked into hell, now could I, Miss?'

The woman wore a strange smile that wasn't reassuring.

'What should I do now? I'm afraid, and I ruined the

chair. I'll lose my job, my home.'

'You can get another job. You can make another home, far from this cursed place.'

'Are... are you Maggie? Maggie McIntyre? The falsely accused?'

'Yes and no. I am Maggie McIntyre but the accusation of witchcraft was fair not false.'

'You made that thing?' Laura pointed to the now inanimate sofa.

'I enchanted it. This is the Salon of Lost Souls and it is no place for the living to venture at night. Don't wait until morning. Leave now. Change your name. Hide. But whatever you do, don't come back here.'

Laura nodded. The job, the money, none of them was worth this. 'How many ghosts are here?'

'Hundreds,' Maggie answered. 'Each month more join us. It's like a waiting room for the dead, this place. The unlucky ones end up in hell, the not quite so unlucky ones stay here. We argue. We fight. We fuck and sometimes we play hide and seek with wee Master Robert. You've met Master Robert. He was most put out that you wouldn't play.'

'I'm sorry.'

'Don't be. If you had played I would have needed to save you sooner. He doesn't play fair.'

'Thank you, Maggie.'

'You can thank me by getting away and staying safe.'

The apparition faded into the shadows. Laura stumbled toward her apartment and packed her bags. What was too large to take in the car was left. She placed the apartment key on the shop counter before she locked the house door behind her. At least the staff would have the opportunity to see the apartment now, before another poor, lost soul took the job.

Impatient for Death, a Love Story
TW: Suicide attempts

Chloe held her lover's face in her mind. A pale and beautiful face. Kind and patient eyes of a blue so deep they were almost indigo. The face was not strictly male or female, but the finest of both. A soft mouth with rosebud lips that Chloe yearned to kiss. A square jaw and a finely sculpted nose that never looked haughty.

She held a knife in her trembling but determined hand. Fragrance from rose petals, which floated lethargically on the warm water, caressed her senses. The bathtub and sharp blade promised a beautiful death.

Chloe tested the temperature with her toe, perfect. Petals tickled her skin as she lowered herself into the bath. Eager turquoise veins presented themselves on her forearm. She rested the blade centimetres above her left wrist. Gentle fingers wrapped around her right hand, holding her back.

'Kiss me,' Chloe begged. Tears blurred her vision.

'Not yet. Be patient,' her lover replied.

Chloe was fourteen when her mother finally died. She had watched the woman grow weaker, twisted by pain from doting parent to hollow shell for three years before it happened. Chloe was at her mother's bedside when she drew her final breath. That was the first time she saw her lover, knelt beside the deathbed of a beloved but cancer tortured parent.

Her mother saw it too. Dressed in the darkest black Chloe had ever seen, pale skin shining like moonlight in contrast. Soft lips moved as words were whispered too quietly for Chloe to hear. Then it happened. The mask of pain slipped. Her mother's bright eyes shone with passionate desire. A desire shared by the lover by the nature of their kiss. A kiss so potent her mother's body shuddered then went completely still. A kiss that remained vivid in Chloe's memory. The kiss she wanted from her lover as they held her knife-wielding hand but denied her request. Told her to be patient.

'When?' Chloe no longer felt beautiful. Her face was creased with frustration. Tears of anger blotched her skin. Her nakedness was ugly, not perfect. 'When?' she shouted.

The hand withdrew from hers and the knife tumbled into the water, slicing her thigh. She sucked air through her teeth. A thread of crimson blossomed among the petals.

'I can't tell you that, but you have a life to lead first. This is not your time, Chloe.'

Her lover had denied her. He was cruel with his rejection, like her father who ran from the cancer diagnosis, leaving

Chloe alone with the dying and the dead. At that moment Chloe mentally attached a male gender to Death. The deep timbre of his voice as he disappointed her seemed to fit the arbitrary gender assignment. She saw other things to support her supposition, large hands, flat chest and long limbs. She wasn't sure whether he accepted the label. In his presence she continued to address him as "you", "my love" or sometimes, to be mischievous, "sir". He always frowned when she called him that, but then she hadn't seen him smile since that day at her mother's bedside. The day he stole Chloe's heart.

Chloe chain smoked. Her friends berated her for it. 'Those'll kill you, you know.'

'Not soon enough.'

So she flirted with other drugs, but the empty eyes of junkies never held the same attraction for her. The only thing they loved was oblivion and she was certain that wasn't what she was chasing.

She rode a motorbike, taking corners at break-neck speed. Blindly overtaking cars and lorries. She was a risk taker and only the metal pins, put in her shin after a nasty accident, prevented her from continuing along those roads.

She wore her scars proudly, testament to her nihilistic excesses. Only one of them really reminded her of him. The scar on her thigh from the knife in the bathtub. She guarded that memento jealously, angered if anyone noticed it.

Chloe knew she couldn't die in a bathtub now. He would be disappointed. Repetition revealed a lack of imagination. She needed better ways to attract his attention.

Night stripped the beach of colour. Waves glistened silver at their tips. An incessant roar of pebbles, moving under the surface. Chloe removed her jeans and sweater.

The water was too cold. Ice stabbed her feet, but her skin numbed to the pain as she strode out, skating over loose stones until her feet no longer touched ground. Her heart thumped, trying to keep going. The darkness swallowed her, but still he didn't come.

So cold.

Ice water lapped at her toes. Her blue skin shivered and her teeth chattered so hard she thought they might shatter.

He knelt beside her, a tear rolling down his moonlit cheek. He covered her with his cape and rubbed her skin dry. He had vanished before her teeth had stopped gnashing enough to speak. Another rejection that did nothing to dampen her ardour.

Commuters raced along the asphalt, weaving like salmon into tight spaces to shave a minute off their journeys. At sixty miles per hour or more the impact should kill her instantly. He must come and give her his kiss this time.

Red, black, silver, midnight blue. Painted metal frames rushed past. The disturbed air ruffled her hair. Excitement made her skin tingle. The wait was almost over. She edged forward. A horn blared. She refused to be frightened away from her purpose. In the distance red and blue lights flashed. It was now or never. She closed her eyes and ran.

Metal tore open with an eardrum-splitting screech. Glass exploded. Chloe opened her eyes. A tsunami of vehicles piled onto each other, some mounted the central barrier. Glass shards surrounded her feet and glinted on her clothes. Blood stained her dress, but not her blood. She ran from the scene in horror as sirens wailed. In the passenger seat of a crushed car, her lover kissed another.

The roof tiles were slippery with water. Rain lashed down, punching her face. Shards of light split the sky from black clouds to the trembling earth. Chloe lifted her arms toward heaven and yelled. 'Kiss me now, you bastard.'

He sat beside her, legs straddling the apex of the deep red roof. He stared at her face as she pushed wet hair from her eyes. Clothes clung to her skin. The lightning bolts moved further away. She blushed, feeling suddenly ashamed.

'You always see me at my worst,' she admitted.

He nodded slowly and her heart broke in two.

'Yet I still love you. What does that say about your value?'

'You're disappointed?'

'Of course. All that potential and you waste it chasing thunder clouds.'

'But the kiss.'

'It was never yours to take.'

Chloe fell to her knees and wept. The rain washed away her tears. She was alone again. Carefully she climbed down the ladder and decided on a more noble death.

Death surrounded her. Chloe had never realised the cruelty of her lover until she stepped into a war torn city dressed in her nation's uniform. Men, women and children dead at the roadside. Body parts scattered with no order, no dignity, no lips for Death to kiss and give them peace. The air stank of blood, faeces and lord knew what else. Other soldiers moved around her, picking their way through the bodies, never finding one alive.

As she approached a corner she heard the cries of a child. She hurried towards the sound and found an almost intact play park at the end of the battered street. A kid, no older than six, sat on a swing, feet dragging on the ground, bellowing for his mother.

Between her and the child were less than one hundred

metres of unkempt grass. She jumped over the low fence and ran towards him. His crying grew louder.

'I'm coming,' she shouted in a language he wouldn't understand. Knowing the futility of reaching him in all this carnage, but needing to do it anyway. To do this one good, selfless deed now she was no longer beholden to the god of death. The child was a lifeline. She needed to hold him more than he needed her to save him. This was her purpose and it engulfed her.

The pins in her shin throbbed each time she landed on her right leg, but the pain was good. It reminded her that she was still alive, and where there was life, surely there was hope.

Her foot sank into the grass. Surrounded by blinding white light, she shot into the air. She was flying. Her body ripped apart. Legs and arms tumbling through the smoke filled sky in different directions.

He was there. Death. He held her head and chest in his arms. That was all that remained of her body now. A landmine she guessed. His lips came closer. The kiss.

'You monster!' she screamed. 'What have you done?'

'Forgive me, Chloe.'

'Forgive you? Never. You're twisted. All this time. All these beautiful deaths you denied me. What about the boy? You let me care. You let me choose life, for what? No! This isn't fair. My lover is not this cruel. He cannot be. I've not been chasing a monster all these years. No! My mother loved you. I loved you. No, no, no! Please no. Don't you dare fucking kiss me now.'

His tears covered her face, a waterfall of suffering, but she could not forgive him. She died trying to escape his kiss.

Jagged Jaws

TW: Sexual assault, drugging, herbal tea

'Do you remember Daryl Smith?' Clare asked, handing me a cup of fruit tea.

In spite of all the years, fear and disgust slapped my face.

'Are you okay?' she asked. 'You look as though you're about to throw up.'

I forced myself to nod. This wasn't a conversation I was ready to have, not twenty years after the event and probably not after fifty years. The shame of it had burrowed its roots deep into my psyche. The packed soil, of experiences since that I'd used to insulate me from the pain, shook and cracked when I heard his name again. All that work rebuilding myself had never gained any solidity. The foundations were as shaky as ever.

'What about him?' My voice sounded thin, insubstantial.

Clare glared at me. The weight of her stare pinned me, squirming on the kitchen stool. Did she know?

'He got married. They're expecting a baby.'

Daryl was in Clare's year at school. I'd been in the

year above. We'd all left that concrete-blocked structure decades ago, but I guessed she'd kept in touch.

Daryl had been a friend of my school sweetheart. He was a troubled kid from a trouble-making family with a pleasant face and saccharine charm. Although it was hard to recall his facial features clearly, I remembered dark hair, tanned skin and roguish good looks. When I pictured him it wasn't his face that sprang to mind, it was a part of him that hung midway between head and ludicrously expensive trainers.

I wanted to be alone, to stamp on these memories and trample them deeper, but I was cradling a freshly made cup of rhubarb tea and Clare had been bugging me for weeks to meet up for a chat. I couldn't simply leave, not without explaining why.

'They've got a croft in Thorne village. It's a lovely place. She's a landscape gardener. Although, I guess she'll need to take it easy for a while, have more of a managerial role.'

I stared at the pink liquid in my cup, pretending to care, but a reply wouldn't form in my throat. Clare's chatter tightened its grip on me, squeezing. My mouth was full and I was choking.

'Anyway, they're having a party the weekend after next. I can bring a guest. Do you wanna come? There might be lots of the old crowd there. Maybe Stuart. They're still friends. Daryl was talking about Stuart the other day. He's single. He works for the MOD. Apparently he's still gorgeous...'

I couldn't hate her. She was trying to be sweet. I guess she'd watched me sprint through relationships since school, with long fallow periods between, and assumed I was still in love with the boy I'd lost at fifteen.

It wasn't her fault that I'd never trusted her enough to tell her why I found sustaining adult relationships an impossible task. She was supposed to be my best friend, but really she knew nothing about me. She couldn't understand my rage.

'Aww come on. It'll be fun. It'll be like old times.'

'Excuse me,' I said, grasping my stomach and fleeing for the bathroom.

I can't remember exactly how Clare convinced me to go, but here I was feeling shabbily dressed outside a rather grand stone cottage. My only consolation was that Clare was doing a superb impression of the Cheshire cat beside me. I'd rarely seen her so excited.

Can you call someone a best friend if you only have one friend? My life had become so tiny over the years that I had all my fun by proxy, listening to her stories. I knew all her disappointments. Her volatile relationships with work colleagues, the lovers who failed to call, and the ones who wouldn't stop calling. It was refreshing to see her face without any shadow of sadness; it almost made me forget my own for a moment.

The door was ajar. I guessed this was the sort of area where you didn't have to lock up your bargain-basement possessions for fear of theft. The music wafting into the garden was as bouncy as my friend. I gripped a chilly bottle of Lambrusco tighter in my fist and stepped inside.

It was busy. Half-remembered faces mingled with strangers as Clare and I wove between them toward the kitchen to drop off our bottles and greet our hosts. My saliva tasted metallic. Would Daryl recognise me? Would I recognise him? Who else would I know at this party and could I depend on Clare to stick beside me this time? One thing I knew for certain, I'd be mixing my own drinks this evening.

A beautiful couple rested against a polished oak workstation at the centre of the kitchen. Between making drinks and smiling graciously at guests they pawed at each other's arms and gazed into each other's eyes. The wide-smiled, floppy-haired, pretty boy was unmistakably Daryl. The woman, presumably his wife, had flame coloured tight curls and golden freckles on her heart shaped face. Her clothing and posture were effortlessly elegant but strong. The only hint of softness, other than her kind eyes, was the curve of her belly shielding the undoubtedly healthy baby growing within.

The woman glanced across at us and waved. 'Clare.'

'Hi, Amanda ... Daryl. Great party. Congratulations. We brought some wine. This is Pam. Do you remember Pam?'

The name and my face did not invoke any sign of recognition. The smiles were professional, like photographs of catalogue models in a family setting. It was hard to believe he didn't recognise me at all. I wanted to growl something at him, but kept silent.

'Can I get you drinks?' Daryl asked.

I shuddered and saw again the mug of cola in my hand.

'Red please?' Clare answered.

'... Pam?' Daryl asked. Staring at my face as if trying to recall who I was.

I shook my head. 'I'm fine thanks.'

Clare reached out and squeezed my hand, reassuringly.

Neither Amanda nor Daryl lost their smiles.

'You must show ... Pam the garden, Clare. We'll catch up with you later.'

'It's Amanda's showcase garden. Her pride and joy. She uses it to display her talents to prospective clients. It's even better in daylight,' Clare gushed as we stepped outside.

Fairy lights twinkled in the trees and yellow stone pathways guided feet between closely cropped, lush lawns.

The fragrance from flowers, heavy and sweet, gave a magical feeling to this place as though we'd accidentally stepped over the rainbow into Oz or fallen down a rabbit hole into Wonderland. I was enchanted. For a moment I let my guard slip and was happy.

'Clare ... Pam?'

I saw sparkling green eyes and recognised him immediately.

'Stuart.' The ground moved beneath my feet. His hair was darker than the ash blond I remembered - a light brown with soft highlights that might or might not have been natural. I hadn't seen him in twenty years, but I had never forgotten his smile. I could drown in it. 'Long time, no see.'

'Oh my god. It is you? How have you been?'

I nodded. 'Busy. You?'

'Oh you know.'

I didn't but I nodded anyway.

Amanda grinned at me. 'I'll just be a minute. You guys can keep each other company, right?'

'I'll take good care of her,' Stuart said, but his eyes looked predatory.

He made my skin tingle, just by standing there. His eyes only left my face for seconds to appraise the rest of me before returning, the trademark mischievous sparkle had not faded.

'You look good,' I told him.

'You too. How long has it been?'

'Nineteen years and eleven months.' My reply was instant. 'Not that I've been counting.'

'You haven't changed a bit,' he said.

'Oh I have,' I replied.

He glanced over his shoulder. 'Daryl and Amanda have a lovely place. Have you been here before?'

'No. Clare brought me.'

His nod was so slight I might have missed it if I hadn't been staring.

'Want a guided tour?'

He showed me the garden first, Amanda's magnus opum - there was a well-stocked shed, unlocked, with walls full of gardening tools that reminded me of instruments of torture. I considered for a moment what that said about me. The summer house and barbecue, currently unused, stood beside a pond full of koi carp, surrounded by ornamental reeds and grasses. It was heavenly. I imagined sitting here on summer days with kids racing around behind me on tricycles or roller-skates. Sadness stabbed my chest. I'd never have this. It was my mirage in a desert.

He held my hand when we entered the busy house, my palm sweaty in his soft grip. Everything inside had been as carefully planned as the garden. I wondered how a toddler's crayon scribbles across these pale walls would be received. Maybe Amanda would redecorate before that time came.

Three bedrooms, including one in the process of having its wallpaper stripped - nesting. I remembered the last time Stuart and I had been together. That first time, which became the last time and a fat tear rolled down my cheek.

'I'm so sorry, Pam. I was a kid.'

'So was I.'

He squeezed my hand. 'I know.'

We turned to leave the room and the memory behind us.

'Pam?'

'Yes.'

'Would you ...'

I waited, but he didn't continue. 'What?'

'Can I take you to dinner?'

'So what did you say?' Clare asked.

I shrugged. 'What could I say?'

'A thousand different things, but I hope you said yes.'

I nodded. 'Yes ... I did.'

She made a high pitched squeal and wrapped her arms around me. 'That's wonderful. I'm so excited for you. We need to buy you a new dress ... and shoes ... maybe you should get your hair done.'

'Slow down.'

'I'm just excited for you.'

She took the kettle to the sink and filled it. It was our ritual, drinking tea together, fruit tea normally. She thought it was good for us, cleansing. God knows I needed a good cleanse.

'Really? Coz I'm fucking terrified.'

She cocked her head and stared at me for a moment, before switching the kettle on. 'Why?'

'Because I think I still love him and that scares the shit out of me.'

'It'll be fun. It's exactly what you need.'

I couldn't grasp how this feeling could ever be described as fun. It was like waking up from a nightmare and not knowing whether I was still dreaming. Hot, sweaty and sick, it wasn't fun at all. It was torture.

Stuart had broken my heart when he was fourteen and I was fifteen. Whether it was Stuart's betrayal or what followed that royally fucked me up, I wasn't quite sure. How different would my life have been if I'd never met Stuart or Daryl? It would have to be better than this. Yet here I was, entering the lion's den once more, only this time my eyes were wide open.

'When?' Clare poured boiling water into two mugs. This time mine had a striped cat with razor claws and a green and red sweater.

'You have such cool cups.' I stared at the fruit tea and sniffed. 'Blackberry?'

She nodded.

The water was dark, like thin blood.

'When are you having dinner?'

I sighed. 'Saturday.'

'You have to tell me all about it.'

'I can tell you now. We'll eat. We'll talk about old times and we'll leave each other both feeling absolutely rotten. Why am I doing this again?'

Clare appeared confused. 'I understand the nostalgia, but why feel rotten? It doesn't have to be an ending.'

'I can't ...' The words wouldn't come. The memory had frozen part of my heart. That's probably the only reason it had endured, stayed fresh even. My love for him had been cryogenically preserved. The love that he had pissed all over. I'd been naïve, innocent and I had thought he meant it when he said he loved me. Now I had no faith in those words.

'What happened between you?'

'Don't you know?'

'I just thought you broke up. Is there something else?'

'He called me a slut.'

'Oh, Pam ... He was fourteen. It won't be like that now.'

Once the words came I couldn't stop them tumbling from my jagged jaws. 'He was my first. I loved him. Fuck, we'd been going out for two years before ... After, he wouldn't talk to me. He talked to everyone else though. Told them what we'd done. Said I was easy. Said I was a slut. I was fifteen.'

'He didn't mean it. People say stupid things. He was probably as confused as you were. I know he hurt you. Maybe it's time to put it behind you. Maybe this is the closure you need ... to move on ... with or without Stuart. You know you're not a slut.'

'I know that now.'

'Oh Pam.' She stood up and walked around the table, wrapped me inside her arms and hugged me. My cheek squashed the cushions of her breasts. 'Poor baby. I didn't know. I hadn't heard. It's history now right. Don't cling onto it. You'll be better off without it. Give him a second chance, okay.'

'You don't understand.'

'Then tell me. Explain.'

'I can't. I'm too ... ashamed.'

'You're not the first woman or girl to be called a slut, Pam, and you certainly won't be the last. Fuck their women-hating crap. We're too good for all that shit. You have to let it go. It was twenty years ago.'

Slut – Stuart hadn't been the only boy to call me that. Daryl did too. Stuart said it because I said yes. Daryl because I'd said no. Clare was right. It was a word used to communicate hatred, to make someone feel worthless. The trouble was I did feel worthless. I still felt worthless. Sometimes words had an awful lot of power.

I held my face over the steam that rose from the blackberry tea. The word was one symbol, the mug another. I told Clare about the word, but not about the mug or what had followed. That was a secret I would carry to my grave.

Saturday came too quickly. I hadn't prepared myself for its arrival. Clare had chosen my dress, but I didn't wear it. I wore trousers and a blouse, like armour, and flat shoes.

Stuart was already at the table and he stood up as he watched me approach. The smile appeared again and I was lost. I glanced down at my plain clothes and wished I'd been brave enough to don the figure-hugging dress. He didn't seem to notice. His eyes were on my face as it mirrored his welcoming grin.

We sat simultaneously and my knee brushed against his. I buried my face in the menu as my cheeks ripened. How could anyone be this awkward at 35? It was pathetic. It wasn't like I hadn't had my fair share of first dates. I just hadn't had many second ones, and for the life of me I couldn't figure out what this was. Could past lovers have first dates?

A shadow hovered beside me and I shivered, but it was only the waiter.

'Would you like wine?' Stuart asked.

'White please,' I replied.

Stuart read a French name from the menu and the waiter nodded and withdrew.

'I don't know what to choose.' I grinned awkwardly.

'Are you still vegetarian?'

I looked up from the menu. He remembered. I nodded slowly.

'The roasted vegetable lasagne is supposed to be excellent. I'm afraid I'm still a carnivore. Do you mind?'

'I'll have the lasagne. Thank you. Do you come here often? Wow that was cheesy.' I giggled self-consciously.

'Before I became a bit of a hermit, it was a fairly regular haunt. It's near work.' He reached across the table and brushed my thumb with his. 'Guess what?'

That one sentence ...

We sat together in the youth club. Nineties pop blaring. We had just shared our first kiss. His cheek was touching mine and he whispered the words in my ear. 'Guess what?'

'What?'

'I love you.'

I nodded.

'I've been really nervous about tonight. I managed to convince myself you wouldn't come, not that I'd blame you.' Stuart's nervous stammer endeared me to him even more.

I continued to nod as his words washed over me. He was right. I shouldn't have come. Yet, when I tried to stand up and leave, my muscles would not obey the request and I continued to sit, nodding, like one of those toy dogs on the back shelves of cars. Nodding, nodding, unable to stop.

'I thought about contacting you lots of times.'

Nod.

'I was just a stupid kid, but ...'

Nod.

'I really did love you.'

A tear pushed under my lashes and rolled down my cheek. He grasped my hand.

'Shhh, don't cry.'

I brushed the tear away, denying my grief.

The shadow returned and a hand showed us a bottle. Now Stuart was nodding. Glug, glug, the wine was poured into my glass. I picked it up and downed the liquid. It warmed my throat even though the Chardonnay was chilled. The waiter refilled my glass.

'Are you ready to order?' His French accent was syrupy.

'Ummm ... vegetable lasagne please.'

'Steak, rare with a pepper sauce.'

'Fillet or Sirloin, sir?'

'Sirloin.'

'Very good. Is the wine to your satisfaction?'

'Yes thank you,' I answered before Stuart replied. I wanted the waiter to leave Stuart and me alone, but I wanted him to stay, so I wouldn't start weeping again.

I didn't know what to say to Stuart, the one person I had truly loved, who had betrayed me and in doing so caused all the evil of my life to unfold. I wished I had never met him, but if I hadn't I wouldn't still remember those soft lips against mine, every time I heard the right song.

'I see.'

'What do you see?' he asked, squeezing my hand again. His face framed a smile that could melt the Arctic tundra.

'You were a stupid kid. We were both stupid kids and this is a mistake.'

'Stay for dinner at least. Call it my apology, and if you don't want to forgive me ... Well at least I'll know I tried.'

'I-'

His eyes were kind, as if there was nothing I could ever say that would make him angry. He was so gentle. He had always been ... gentle. He nodded, encouragingly.

'I do want to forgive you.' The words came out with my breath and I inhaled to reclaim them, but it was too late. 'I just don't know whether I can. What you did ... what happened after ... everything bad in my life ...' I wanted to tell him it was all his fault, but it wasn't. It was about time I stopped blaming Stuart for every failed relationship in my adult life and looked elsewhere. 'You said ...'

'I know what I said. I didn't mean it, Pam. I was scared and confused. I pushed you away. It was stupid. But when I tried to speak to you ... well you remember ...'

'I don't,' I whispered.

'Really?'

'I don't remember you speaking to me at all, after ...'

It was his turn to look embarrassed and his cheeks and throat blotched with crimson patches. 'Well, to be honest ... I didn't get as far as talking.'

'What do you want?' My voice was harder than I intended, but it was out, laid bare, like my soul, in front of him.

He emptied his wine glass and his eyes were softer than before as though shrouded by mist, or I was studying him through a smudged lens.

'I want a second chance.'

'Did you say yes?' Clare asked.

'I didn't say no,' I answered, staring vacantly at the cat on my lap who was shedding pale fur all over my clothes.

'When will you see him again?'

'I said I'd call him.'

'And have you?'

'Not yet.'

'What are you waiting for?'

'There's something I need to take care of first.'

'What?'

'I need to feel free.'

'You're not dating anyone. You've been single for months. You are free.'

'I haven't been free for a very long time, Clare.'

'What are you talking about, Pam? You're scaring me. Look at me, not the cat. What do you need to do to feel free?'

'I need to say goodbye.'

'To me?'

'No, don't be silly.'

'I don't understand you when you get into these moods, Pam. I thought you'd be happy. Stuart asks you out again after twenty years, and what ... you're gonna fuck it all up? Grow up. You aren't fifteen anymore.'

'I have to go.' I brushed the cat from my lap and stood up. I left the kitchen, knowing Clare was sat open-mouthed behind me.

'Pam?'

I didn't stop. I left her flat without my jacket. The air was warm anyway and I didn't feel I would need it. I had my handbag, clutched in my fist, with enough money to get where I needed to go. It was going to be okay. I would say goodbye then I would be free. After that it was up to me.

When I arrived at Daryl's I still wasn't sure what I planned. One car was parked in the generous driveway and the house seemed deathly quiet. Perhaps they were both out. I stood in front of their rustic front door and let my mind drift. It travelled back in time and for once I let it.

I was holding that mug again. Cola bubbles spluttered upwards, bursting in the air. I took a sip and then another. The friendly conversations around me became homogeneous noise and I drifted again.

Stuart and I lay on a tangled duvet. His thumb stroked between my legs and I gasped and moaned with pleasure. *Give her the thumb. They like that.* When had I heard those words? Oh yes in the park, from his older brother. We'd been fooling around and my white mini skirt was covered in green stains.

The mug again. I didn't suspect a thing. I hadn't heard of date rape drugs back then. In fact it took me over a decade to accept that what happened that day wasn't my fault.

My head swam and my limbs were impossibly heavy. Maybe I had a migraine coming on. I asked if I could lie down for a while and a friend helped me stumble up the stairs and onto a single bed.

I thought I'd sleep it off. Wake up fresh and apologise.

It wasn't my first migraine, although this seemed different, but I was too muddled to try and work out what was wrong. Sleep ... that's what I needed. I sank into the mattress.

I felt sick. What was I doing here? Was I mad? What did I plan to say if Daryl or, perhaps worse, his wife came to the door. I couldn't tell them about that day. Twenty years and many hours of therapy later and I still didn't have all the pieces. More was conjecture than not. Sometimes I felt sure it had only been a nightmare. But a dream couldn't have haunted me for that long - the shame, the fear, the anger. No, it had happened. He had done that to me. I was a victim and the only way I'd get past this point in my life was to make Daryl pay, in full. I pressed the doorbell.

The door opened. I sensed it more than I saw it. A sharp chill entered the room and I shivered, trying to bury further into the sheets. A movement in the room. My eyes were closed, but a shadow passed across them and I saw the inside of my lids change from red to black then back again. I tried to open my eyes, but the lids were too heavy. The mattress dipped. Someone was sitting beside me, leaning above me. A smell filled my nostrils, sweat and musk. A hand touched my hair. I was trapped. Pinned to a strange bed, unable to see or move, unable even to open my mouth and ask who was there. I was living a nightmare and I couldn't wake up.

'You got away last time,' the male voice whispered.

Got away? I knew at once it was Daryl and remembered a scene I had tried to drive from my mind. It had happened within a week of Stuart's betrayal. A sharp kick and a swift run and it had been left behind. A frightening moment, a warning, but nothing more. At least not until now.

'This time you're stuck here. Just you and me.'

I shook my head, or hoped I was moving it. I would deny him to my final breath. Never surrender.

'You're a filthy slut. Don't pretend you're a virgin. I know what you did.'

Bile rose in my throat. I swallowed, but a lump of it lingered there, burning.

'I'll give you a choice. Suck me or fuck me.'

No answer. I pressed the doorbell again, longer this time. Letting the sound of it break through the words in my head. It was the scream I had not been able to articulate. The scream that might have saved me, or not, depending on who had been left in the house. Maybe it had just been Daryl and me, like he'd claimed. Or maybe help was waiting downstairs for a sign it was needed. Maybe the right noise would have brought footsteps hammering up those stairs.

I decided to check the garden. I'd been told it was

even more beautiful in daylight and that wasn't a lie. Flowers jostled for my attention and bright colours created a powerful display that calmed my mind. The scent of them equally powerful. I wandered towards the shed. It smelled peaty inside, rich, earthy, musky.

The smell of him filled my nostrils and I wanted to vomit. Did he ever wash? He smelled revolting, like old cheese and sweat. Stuart had never smelled like this. His body had been fresh and smelled of soap. Daryl's flesh was rank. His skin pressed against my mouth, prising open my lips. I wanted to bite down hard. I wanted to hear him scream, but my jaw was unwilling or unable to do my bidding. It yielded to his will, not mine, and opened around him.

Tools hung from hooks against the rough wooden wall. Some had black handles, some red and others green. Spades, hoes, forks, shears and secateurs, clean, sharp and oiled, all ready to be used. I could destroy the dream garden, dig up plants, cut blooms from their stems. I would show no mercy. Maybe they would look around them terrified, unsure about what had sparked this wrath. Maybe they would assume it was jealousy, report the damage and move on. Amanda might mourn those wasted hours. Her tears might spill onto parched earth. The thought gave me little satisfaction. Amanda wasn't the person I needed to punish. But there were other ways I could use these tools to make sure I targeted the right victim.

I took my time, handling the tools and weighing in my mind what they might be used for. The rope would be perfect. He should be powerless, unable to move, just like I had been, but what next? How much did I want to hurt him? Did I want him dead?

I wondered how I would tie him up. I could try seducing him, but he might not be interested and I didn't feel like even pretending that I found the arsehole attractive. I didn't have the benefit of being able to access drugs like Rohypnol. What I now knew he had probably slipped into my mug all those years ago. Those weren't the circles in which I travelled. I lifted a heavy shovel off the wall, perhaps an old fashioned whack to the back of the head would suffice.

What would I do after I had punished him? Would I head to see Stuart and resume our relationship or would I return to my hermetic lifestyle? Would I be caught? I might not. I had never been in trouble with the police, so there were no records of my DNA or fingerprints as far as I was aware, but of course Daryl would tell them everything. I couldn't leave him as a witness unless I wanted to spend time locked up. Once again a prisoner to someone else's pleasure.

If I was to do this at all, I had to be willing to kill him.

Could I do that? He might have humiliated me, assaulted me, made me his victim, but should that carry a death sentence?

Here I was in his well-stocked shed, in his beautiful garden, outside the perfect home he shared with his gorgeous and pregnant wife. Daryl had it all. In contrast, I had not been able to maintain a relationship for longer than a week. I couldn't fall asleep beside anyone. I never accepted a drink I hadn't made myself or carefully supervised the making of. I drifted from minimum wage job to minimum wage job. Each evening, I would watch television until my eyes closed rather than retire voluntarily to my bed, and every night I woke up screaming, afraid to fall back to sleep and leave myself vulnerable again. I was in hell and Daryl, perhaps with Stuart's help, had sent me there. He did not deserve a moment longer in this paradise. I would do it. I would make him powerless and then I would kill him. If Amanda returned too soon I would slaughter her as well. If not I would let her and the baby continue. No one would suspect me. Only Daryl and I knew my motive and he would carry the knowledge to his cold grave.

I would need a plan, however. Not just waiting in the shed for someone to arrive. It would more likely be Amanda who came here first, after all it was her shed and her tools I had decided to co-opt as weapons. Plus, the one car left on the driveway might mean they would arrive home together.

The super-fit, gardening-crazy wife, even with child, would be stronger than me. They both would. Against the two of them I wouldn't stand a chance.

I returned the shovel to its hook and left the shed. The sun was still high in the sky. I checked my watch. It was four o'clock. Daryl might still be at work and Amanda could be anywhere doing anything. What I needed was some reconnaissance. I would study them, learn their habits, but to do that I'd need warmer clothes and a lot of patience. I decided to return the following day.

'So?' Clare asked as she opened the door to let me in.

'So what?' I shrugged, dismissively.

'Did you say your goodbyes? Are you free?'

I glanced at the floor. If I told her I wasn't she'd keep asking questions and eventually she might start discussing my weird behaviour with her friends. Perhaps even with Daryl and Amanda. If I told her I was she'd expect me to call Stuart and say yes to our next date. I wished I hadn't returned to her flat, but I'd left my jacket there and I'd need it tomorrow. It wasn't as though I owned more than one.

'Yes.'

She grinned. 'Have you phoned him?'

'Stuart? Not yet.'

'Want to use my phone? Save the credit on yours.'

I chewed my lip and she glanced at me askew.

'Don't tell me you're having second thoughts, already.'

'I don't know why it matters to you who I date, Clare.'

'It doesn't, not really. But you don't date anyone. You seem so lonely. So sad. You're my friend, Pam. I really think this will be good for you. You just have to be brave enough to try.'

'I don't know him. It was twenty years ago.'

'That's what dates are for, silly. To get to know people. I'm not suggesting you should marry him.' She laughed as if she'd told the funniest joke ever.

I laughed along and put my hand out for her phone. 'Do you have his number?'

'Yeah, hang on, it should be in the address book. She studied the screen and highlighted a name and number. Here,' she said, handing it across.

All I had to do was press the phone icon and I would be ringing him. I didn't know what I'd say, but I supposed that didn't matter. Most people probably didn't script phone calls to old friends. My thumb hovered over the button. It was shaking, no, I realised my entire body was shaking. Clare smiled at me as if this was completely normal. I decided to sit down. Her eyes followed me, then she seemed to decide I might need privacy and left me alone at her kitchen table to make my call.

I pushed gently on the button.

'Hello?'

'Hi Stuart. It's Pam.'

'Hi. I was worried you wouldn't call. I'm sorry dinner was a bit awkward. I didn't mean to put you on the spot. You kind of left too quickly for me to apologise. I should have called, maybe. Or maybe I shouldn't. Was I right to give you space?'

I smirked at his nervous voice. 'Yes.'

'Oh good. I never know what's for the best.'

You always used to. Did something happen to change you too?

'It's okay. About Saturday ...'

'Yes?'

'We could do something. Perhaps during the day.'

'That would be great. Shall I pick you up? Where do you live these days? I'm guessing not with your parents anymore.'

'It's okay. I'll meet you. Name a coffee shop in the city centre. Shall we say two o'clock?'

He paused. 'Do you know the Italian coffee shop in the mall?'

'I'll see you there. If you get there first I take mine black no sugar.'

'Got it.'

I pressed the phone icon again and placed the mobile gently on the table. I didn't realise I'd made a sound, but perhaps it was the break in conversation that summoned Clare back to the kitchen.

'I'm so proud of you Pam. What are you going to wear?'

~

This time when I rang on Daryl's door he opened it. Again there was only one car on the drive and I'd wrongly assumed the house was empty. Ringing the doorbell was as much habit as precaution.

He looked at me without the slightest recognition in his eyes. Perhaps I had dreamed the party, or he only had eyes for his wife these days. I chose to play on his poor memory.

'Is Amanda there?' I asked.

'No. She won't be back until six.'

'She asked me to check the azaleas. Is it all right if I go ahead?'

He appeared puzzled for a moment then nodded. 'Sure ... Do I know you?'

'I'll leave you to figure that one out while I check on the flowers. Come and find me when you have.' It was a risk. He might phone his wife to confirm my identity, but the sparkle in his eyes suggested he approved of my game.

He nodded. 'Tea or coffee?'

'Tea please. Should I come in for it when I've

finished?'

'Sure. I'll leave the door open.'

The shed waited for me, unlocked as always. These people were so trusting. Had nothing bad ever happened to them? Well that would change soon. I doubted whether, after today, Amanda would be able to leave a single door unlocked. I still hadn't decided what I'd do if she came home too early. I had four hours and that should be plenty of time, but what if her plans changed and I was forced to think fast? Would I hurt her? I didn't know and hoped I wouldn't have to find out. Daryl deserved what was going to happen, I knew that in the deepest parts of me, but Amanda was innocent, or as innocent as anyone in this sick and twisted world, and that baby ...

I lifted the shovel off the hook, some rope, an evil-looking pair of shears and a ridiculously sharp pair of secateurs. I considered each in turn – the spade for the initial blow, or two, or however many it took to knock him out, hopefully without killing him. The rope for tying him up so he would be helpless when he regained consciousness, and the gardener's scissors, both pairs, for snipping, cutting, biting. I wished I'd had the strength to bite him before. Hurt him, crushed him, pierced his skin rather than letting him use my mouth for his pleasure. This time it would be very different. This time my jaws would not be pliant, they would be jagged.

I took the shovel into the house, but left the other tools on the doorstep. I figured I'd be able to explain away one tool. After all I was a gardener, right? He was in the kitchen, sat on the counter again, sipping from a steaming mug.

'So what's your diagnosis?' he asked, nodding towards a mug beside him that would never be tasted.

'Sick.'

'Amanda will be disappointed. Are you uprooting them? You know the tools should be left outside right?'

I stared at him. 'Remember yet?'

He slipped off the counter and stood before me. Like a cornered animal he seemed to be puffing himself up to appear as large and intimidating as possible, but that charming smile never wavered. It chilled me. He shook his head and lifted the second mug, holding it towards me. 'You got me. You'll have to tell me.'

With my left hand I took hold of the mug and threw the hot liquid at his face. The blade of the spade I thrust down hard on his bare foot. He bent forward and I swung the shovel in a wide arc, behind me then over my shoulder, hitting the back of his head before he straightened his body. The blow wasn't truly central and I cut his left ear with the edge of the blade. He dropped to the floor. Blood pooled in his earlobe, his body shook, but he was still conscious and trying to get back up. So I hit him again.

'You're awake,' I said.

He shook his head. His mouth hung open and drool dripped onto his chin. He seemed to struggle to focus on my face. He was on his knees. I'd used the rope to tie his wrists to his legs and around his waist. I tied the knots tightly, restricting his movements to twitches.

'You hit me,' he said in a slow measured tone as if trying to solve a math problem. 'Why am I tied up? What did I ever do to you?'

'You stole my power to say no,' I told him.

He stared at me, then the soft light of recognition danced in his eyes.

'Remember now?' I asked.

'You were Stuart's girl.'

I nodded.

'Shit!'

He struggled against his bondage, tugging at the ropes and testing the knots. I let him. After a few minutes he stopped and sat still.

'What can I say?' he asked.

'Silence would be golden, but you can sob and plead if you want.'

He shook his head and that smile returned. If anything he was more confident than ever. It made me want to crush his skull.

'Amanda will be home soon,' he said, calmly.

'Not for another three hours,' I replied.

'You're pissed at me. I get it. But what are you going to do? Do you want me to apologise? Of course I'm sorry. I was a dumb kid. I was experimenting. I didn't expect you to be so ...'

'Easy?' I swallowed my scream.

'I was going to say docile, subdued, but maybe you're right. Maybe you didn't want to resist. Stuart told me ...'

'I don't want to hear what that wanker told you!' I screamed. 'Shut your fucking mouth or I'll fill it.'

He nodded. He wasn't afraid of me. He was tied up. His head must have hurt like hell, his cheek was swollen and his ear still bleeding, but I saw no trace of fear in his eyes or smile.

I picked up the secateurs and brandished them in front of his face, hoping for some acknowledgement that I had the power. He was at my mercy and I really wasn't feeling merciful.

'You need to put this all back before Amanda arrives,' was all he said.

I screeched in frustration. I wanted him to beg, plead, tell me, while choking back tears, that he was sorry, but he gave me nothing.

I paced the room. Glancing down from time to time. Each time I would catch him wriggling his arms, trying to get free, but he would freeze the moment my eyes settled on him and smile up at me like a trusting child wondering what the next part of the game might be.

I strode across the room towards him and stabbed the metal points into his cheek.

His neck muscles strained as he tried to move back; his eyes grew wider and, for a moment, I felt gratified until I heard his unshakeable voice, still the epitome of calm and reason. 'Be careful with those,' he said. 'They aren't toys.'

'Why aren't you afraid?' I asked him.

'You're owed your little tantrum. I figured I should let you get it out of your system so we can talk.'

'What? I'm going to kill you.'

He pursed his lips before shaking his head slowly. 'No you're not.'

'I fucking am,' I said. 'You raped me.'

'I did not!'

'You drugged me and stuck your penis in my mouth. Oh and by the way, you stank, you should fucking bathe once in a while.'

'You wanted me. I just made it easier for you. You still want me. Come on. I'm helpless. Why don't you come and sit on my lap.'

'How can you say that? When you tried to rape, yes rape, me that first time, on the building site, I kicked you in the balls. You had to fucking ruffie me to get anywhere.

That's rape you asshole.'

'I gave you a choice.'

'I was virtually unconscious.'

'Not so unconscious that your eyes didn't beg me to come to you, that your lips didn't moisten at the thought of my flesh between them.'

'You sick bastard. I'll show you what I think of your cock.'

I rushed at him again. This time I sliced through the denim that covered his lap. He wouldn't stop grinning so I elbowed him in the mouth. That shit eating smile returned immediately even though blood coated his teeth. I dropped the secateurs and put my hands over my ears. I knelt before him, terrified of the power he still wielded.

'It's okay,' he said. 'I understand.'

'You really don't.' I sobbed.

'Let's end it now. Untie me. Leave before Amanda gets home. You can come back tomorrow, earlier, give us more time to play.'

I shook my head. 'Shut up!'

'I can see if Stuart wants to join in too.'

'Shut up! Shut up!'

'A reunion.'

'Shut the fuck up!'

I didn't know what to do. I wanted to run away. No, I wanted to use the shovel to smash in his skull. No, I wanted to cut his dick off and stuff it in his own mouth. I just knelt there, staring through hate-filled eyes at his idiot smile and unfailing self-love. I almost wished Amanda would return so at least this moment would be over. I would be dragged from this hell and into caged safety. How was he so unafraid, so cocksure?

I leaned forwards, so my forehead rested against his chest. I reached for the secateurs and uncovered his crotch. I moved back a little to let him see his small, unthreatening penis asleep on his testicles. It wasn't a weapon. It wasn't a god. It was a pathetic worm.

'If you cut a worm into two, both halves survive,' I said softly, more to myself than him.

He wriggled, trying again to pull his hands free of the ropes.

'I'm not afraid of you,' I told his flaccid penis.

The wriggling grew more urgent. Perhaps Daryl sensed a change in me that made him uncomfortable. I squeezed the handle of the secateurs and its jaws closed around empty air. His body jerked as he struggled more desperately.

I lifted the head of his cock and held it between the thumb and forefinger of my left hand. The fucking pervert got hard. Even now he was excited.

I saw before me every evil deed that men had committed against women – every rape, every child bride, every acid burn, every stoning. I held all this wickedness between my finger and my thumb. I'd uproot it. I let my right hand relax and the jaws of the gardener's tool opened.

'No,' he whispered. 'Please.'

It was a tight fit but I managed to push his member between the hungry metal jaws. His eyes were wide with fear and disbelief. I squeezed. My ears rang with the echoes of his scream.

So much blood. A laugh bubbled in my stomach, rose through my chest and escaped my lips. Daryl was silent now. His head drooped as if he was staring at his crimson thighs. His body shook, but it was impossible to tell whether he was still conscious.

So much blood. I left footprints of it across the kitchen floor. I checked my watch. If Amanda returned at six she would arrive in just under an hour. I'd never clean this mess in that time. The jerking movements of Daryl's chest and stomach had slowed down, but blood still flowed from his raw wound. He would bleed out soon.

I realised I was holding something soft in my left hand. I glanced at the purple flesh and dropped it onto the vinyl, repulsed. Disembodied, it looked uglier than ever. The secateurs were still clutched in my right fist. They would be covered in prints. I dropped them into the sink and filled it with hot water rubbing the taps after. I had to go. The house was remote enough that Daryl's scream, however piercing, should not have been heard. Even if it was, I was boring, non-descript. Witnesses wouldn't recall my features. Daryl hadn't.

I was mesmerised by the gentle twitches of Daryl's shoulders. The blood was slowing, pooling on the floor, reflecting the afternoon sun in its dark depths. I shook myself into action. I must leave now.

My clothes were covered in his blood, my hands too, dark and red. Had any splashed on my face? I visited the downstairs bathroom and cleaned myself, leaving stains on the previously pristine cream hand towel. I grabbed a coat from the cupboard before I left and wrapped it around myself. The air was warm and I found myself sweating as I walked away.

I waited in my flat for the police to call. They didn't. I saw the news report. Amanda looked devastated. Reading between the lines, it seemed she was the prime, if not only, suspect. Poor woman.

The ringing of my phone startled me. This was it. I knew I couldn't escape the consequences of my actions. People like me didn't get to leave their sins behind them. It had taken the police longer than I expected. Would they phone me though? No they would batter my door to take me. The phone and the crime were unconnected. How? Everything in my life was connected to the murder now. I couldn't escape it in my sleep or even make a cup of tea without seeing the scalding liquid I'd thrown in Daryl's face. Red soaked my vision. I felt like Lady Macbeth, marked by blood as a murderer. If I opened my front door people would see me and know what I'd done. My fridge was empty and I was making short work of the frozen food and tins. Soon I would starve if I didn't find a suitable disguise and take the short walk to the local shop.

The phone. It was still ringing. Whoever it was didn't seem to be giving up too easily. Shaking I lifted it from the table.

'Hello?'

'Pam. How are you? You stood me up.'

It was Stuart. He sounded close to tears.

'I saw the news. I'm sorry,' I told him.

'I can't believe Amanda would do such a thing. They seemed so ... Can I see you?'

I swallowed hard. We had nothing to say to each other. The idea of touching him made me want to throw up.

'I don't think so, Stuart. I have to go.'

I hung up on him, wondering whether I had done the right thing. I thought punishing Daryl would free me, but I was more trapped than ever, unable to leave my flat, unable to drink a mug of tea without seeing Daryl's expiring corpse and the blood. So much blood. But I had been powerful. For a moment I had been a god. I had ended his pitiful existence and he would never hurt a woman again. He wasn't the only person to have hurt me though. *Stuart told me*, the words of a rapist, a self-satisfied prick, a dead man. *What did Stuart tell you?* The blood would never be washed from my soul. What difference would more spilled blood make? I picked up the phone again and dialled Stuart's number.

'Actually, how does one hour sound?'

'Great. Let me know your address ... Pam?'

'No, I'll come to yours.'

This time I chose darker clothes. The kitchen knife fitted neatly into my bag.

Stuart lived in a flat, not much bigger than my own but in a better part of town. This was commuter-ville and the only people wandering around at this time a day were a few mothers pushing baby carriages along deserted streets.

He assured me his family home was more impressive, but with child support it would take him a while to get back on top. I found his apologies confusing and shook my head.

'It's fine.'

'I made some cookies,' he said. 'Want tea or coffee with them?'

'Let me make the drinks,' I said. 'What do you want?'

He nodded. 'Black coffee please.'

As I brought the drinks across to the circular table he

was tipping hot biscuits onto a plate.

'They smell good.'

He beamed with pride. 'I like cooking.'

'The perfect boyfriend, huh?' I teased.

He shrugged. 'My wife didn't think so.'

'What happened?'

He passed me a plate, ignoring the question. 'So you heard about Daryl?'

'Yes. Was he a good friend of yours?'

Stuart nodded again. It looked like his head was wobbly he nodded so frequently. Always acquiescent. I hated him for that. I wanted a row.

'I don't know why Amanda did it,' he said, softly, as if to himself.

'Maybe she didn't.'

'The police aren't investigating anyone else.'

'She still might be innocent.'

'I guess, but hell hath no fury, right?' He pulled a face.

'Indeed.'

'I wish I knew how to apologise to you. I feel like such a shit.'

'Explain it. I never did understand what I did wrong. Why did you break up with me?'

'You didn't do anything wrong,' he assured me.

'Then why? Why did you spread those rumours about me? Do you know what horrors you unleashed?'

He cocked his head. 'Huh?'

'What people do to sluts?'

His face crumpled. His brow creased. The corners of his mouth fell. He looked comical for a moment and I laughed.

His eyebrows lifted and his eyes opened wider, making the lines reverse in on themselves. His mouth was still frowning and I thought he looked ridiculous. I lifted my hand to my lips to catch another giggle before it escaped.

'Are you feeling okay?' he asked.

I stared at the wall. A few photos of two pretty children were pinned to the faded wallpaper.

'It's your fault,' I said.

'What's my fault, Pam.'

'When you use that word ... it means ... public property. Do you understand?'

'I'm sorry, Pam. I'm not sure I understand a word you're telling me.'

'Daryl ...'

Stuart grabbed my arm and spun me round to face him. 'What about Daryl?'

Tears swelled in my eyes. The grief I had been clinging to for twenty years poured out of me. 'He said I deserved it. He called me a filthy slut. He said you told him ...' I never did find out what he had said. 'What did you tell him?'

Stuart backed away. He glanced towards his mobile phone on the kitchen counter beside the oven. I shook my head, warning him not to move. He inched away from me, although his eyes never left my face. What sort of monster had I become that this gentle boy was trying to hide from my anger?

I reached inside my handbag and drew out the knife. His eyes dropped from my face to the weapon in my hand. I saw the pulse in his throat. I heard his thoughts. He knew what I had done and he wasn't accepting any responsibility for my actions. But it was his fault. It was. He'd spread lies about me, made me a pariah, made me public property. He'd had his fun then discarded me like a soiled tissue. Nobody understood my pain. Nobody cared. I would always be alone.

But I wouldn't let him tell any more lies about me. I wouldn't let him pick up that phone and tell the police I was a murderer. It wasn't murder. It was justice. What was the right way to deal with such a spreader of lies?

I lunged at him but he pushed me away. The knife skidded across the vinyl away from my hand. I crawled towards it, but he grabbed my ankles and I fell on my chin, biting my tongue. I spat blood onto his floor then looked over my shoulder. His torso shook violently. He sat on the floor with his phone in his fist. I kicked out and knocked it from his fingers. Then kicked again, busting his nose.

The gentleness left his eyes and he snarled as he loomed above me. Blood from his nose dripped onto my clothes and skin. He held his shaking hand out and grabbed the knife. He stared at me as if he was convinced this was all a dream and any moment he would wake up. My tongue throbbed and the reassuring words I offered flapped around my mouth unintelligible.

'Fuck it,' I cursed.

Rising from the floor I pressed my lips against his. Our blood smeared over each other's mouths. His tongue flicked between my lips and into my mouth. His desire overwhelmed him and he used his weight to push me back to the floor. His tongue probed deeper. I bit down hard. He tried to pull away but my teeth were clamped around his tongue. He was pinned in place by my needle sharp jaws. From the corner of my eye I saw him raise his hand. Too late I remembered he still had my knife. The pain was hot, like a poker had been thrust into my ribs. I shuddered and coughed letting him go and he scuttled across the floor. His tongue hung half out of his mouth, swollen and covered in blood. I closed my eyes and let the black heat of my wound carry me away. A smile crossed my lips as a thought crossed my mind that the word slut wouldn't be formed in that broken mouth for a very long time.

Broken Mirror

TW: Self mutilation, body dysmorpia

Mario faced away from me. His shoulders rose and fell with every breath. I pushed myself out from under the starched covers and padded across to the bathroom.

The full length mirror, hung opposite the bathroom door, attracted my attention. I paused in front of it, flashing a smile and pinching my nipples playfully. I glanced back at my lover. He didn't turn. He didn't seem to notice I had left the bed.

I stretched my long, sinewy legs and twirled gracefully. I admired my ass, still high, and the soft skin of my lower back and upper thighs. I still had it. I still knocked young men out.

After using the bathroom I returned to bed. I pressed my chest against Mario's back. He released a stifled sigh. I stroked his dark hair, still damp with sweat, but he didn't respond. He must be deep in some dream. I hoped he was dreaming of me.

My own dreams, when I returned to them, involved running. Was I chasing someone or being chased? Exhilarating, the freedom of stretching my limbs and racing through long grass. The wind caught my hair. It caressed the strands like a gentle lover.

Sunlight, ripping through a gap in the curtains, woke me. Mario lay motionless. His back still facing me. I touched his shoulder. He was cold, so I tucked the covers around his body before leaving the bed. I opened the window and smoked a cigarette. He didn't stir even when the sunlight hit his face with its full force. I must have exhausted the poor bastard.

I tossed my cigarette butt onto a flat roof, closed the window and drew the curtains. The room darkened. I paced around for a while, wondering whether I should wake Mario, deciding instead to take a shower. I wanted my body to smell fresh, ready for our next embrace.

Again the mirror attracted my attention. Shadows lurked beneath my eyes; purple and black stained my skin. I rubbed them, and dragged fingers through my hair. It used to be longer, but I thought this short cut suited me. It framed my face and brought out the bright blue of my eyes.

I opened the bathroom door. Mirrors followed me here as well. I noticed grey amongst my brown tresses and considered tugging them out, but worried that would only make more appear. I would visit a hairdresser and get them to dye it. I was far too young to look old.

The shower was hot and powerful. It massaged my shoulders and back and ran between my thighs. I thought again of Mario curled up on the bed. I stroked my chest and imagined my hands were his. My fingers strayed over my arms and stomach. I wrapped my arms across my chest and pushed my nails into the skin of my back then stroked the curves of my pert ass. I thought to myself how lucky Mario would be when he eventually awoke.

My hand crept between my thighs. As if struck by a lightning bolt my hand jerked away. I switched off the shower and pulled a towel from the heated rail. My skin pinked as I rubbed it dry. I glanced at the bathroom mirror and looked away.

The bathroom door swung into the room as I pulled the handle. I closed my eyes at first, refusing to see what my fingers had found. Standing there, I slowly opened my eyes. Shadows from my thick lashes and the darkness of the room obscured my vision. I opened my eyes wider. Below my toned stomach, something pink and raw hung from me. I must be dreaming. It wasn't real. I tried to push the stray organ back inside my body. It hurt like hell but I kept pushing and punching. I knew that this should not be hanging there. It should be inside me. Veins pulsed along its length. I didn't understand at all. It must be an intestine. I searched for a wound, trying to understand how my insides were outside, but I found no break in my flesh.

I shook my head. The thing was still there, hanging from my abdomen, mocking my attempts to heal myself. It twitched like a rattlesnake preparing to strike. What was it? How did it get there?

Panicked, all I thought about was how to remove this alien creature from my body before Mario awoke. I grabbed my bag from the shelf and hunted through it. Pulling out a t-shirt, underpants, my wallet, I spilled its guts just as my own had been spilled in the shower. My fingers found something hard and cold, and I drew a large pair of scissors from my bag. I couldn't remember why I packed them, perhaps to repair clothing or trim my nails? Whatever my reasons for placing them there, I was glad to find them. They would rid me of this monster.

I put my thumb and index finger through the heavy rings and opened the blades. Yes, these would be large enough. My other hand shook as I dared to touch that thing, the intestine or serpent, whatever protruded from my pelvis. I expected it to be slippery or scaly, but it felt like normal skin, perhaps slightly softer than my hand. I pulled it out in front of me, placed the scissors so the blades were either side then pushed the rings together, making a fist. My scream echoed around the room. So much pain. Shaking and tired, I crawled towards the bed. I called to Mario, but he didn't answer. Blood splattered my thighs and soaked the carpet beneath me. I left my red snail-trail from mirror to bed as a lingering proof of my presence. When I reached the edge of the divan, it took all the strength of my shuddering arms to pull myself up.

I rolled Mario towards me. His eyes remained closed. His mouth bruised and broken. I tugged at the duvet to uncover his body. The same bruises stained his chest, ribs and stomach. Memories flooded into my mind and I tried to swim away. I was drowning in my own violence.

I had met Mario at a street corner and brought him here. He had fucked me. I remembered that. I enjoyed it. But he called me something? What was it? A John. My mind descended into black, then red. I'd lashed out, punching until his screams had been silenced. He lay there, afterwards, faced away, denying me.

Well, I was no John. I held him in my arms as the world became black again. The bed was warm and wet. I sank into its womb-like, tomb-like caress.

154

Dead aHead

TW: Death of infant

Eleanor sat on the sofa, surrounded by empty cola cans and crisp packets. The only source of light was the television, muted so she could hear the soft static hiss of the baby monitor. Beside her a stack of unopened mail threatened to topple and fall. The telephone rang intermittently, always left unanswered. She couldn't remember where her mobile was, but the battery was probably long dead if people were resorting to the land-line to reach out to her.

Obscured by shadows, family portraits clung to the walls, reminders of recent times full of smiles and laughter. The three of them. Before Chris left, or was he evicted? It didn't seem to matter now. It wasn't as though he had tried very hard to return.

Beyond the heavy curtains, a groan of electrical machinery approached. Bin day? Perhaps they would take the dead and dying flowers that crowded around her front door. She would probably need to move them to the gate first, but that would involve opening the door, stepping outside, feeling sunlight on her face, none of which she was ready to do. And what if Rose needed her while she was gone? The baby monitor hadn't communicated anything louder than a soft hum for hours, or was it days, but the moment she left the house even for a second, would be the moment her daughter needed her most. Keeping Rose safe was the only thing that mattered now.

Rose …

Eleanor picked up the pile of letters. Brown envelopes – bills probably, a couple of hand addressed letters, her mother's handwriting, and dozens of squarish envelopes, stiff with cards. She returned them to the coffee table unopened and sucked dregs of flat soda from an open can. Her teeth vibrated as sugar coated them, her breath tasted stale, maybe she was getting sick. The idea exhausted her. Everything exhausted her. She only had room in her head for one thing – Rose.

It was just like Chris to abandon them when they needed him most. Even before he moved out he spent more evenings at work than helping her take care of the baby. She couldn't remember the last time he had changed a nappy or rocked Rose to sleep on fractious nights. He'd escaped the prison of parenthood almost from day one, and left her as sole inmate.

Like that night, a few weeks ago, when Rose had been

feverish. Eleanor had tended to the screaming baby until she was too tired to stand up. Chris' mobile went straight to voicemail. The baby paracetamol did little to calm Rose's distress. Cries bounced off the bedroom walls and echoed through Eleanor's pounding head. It was too loud to think. Should she call a doctor, an ambulance? The surgery thought her overprotective. They hadn't said anything, but she knew. She wanted a second opinion. Someone who would calm her fears or confirm that Rose needed urgent medical care, but Chris wasn't there. No one else was there. It was just Eleanor and the purple-faced monster alone, once again. No monster wasn't fair. Babies cried. It was natural. What wasn't natural was having to do every single fucking thing day after day with next to no sleep. That wasn't natural and Eleanor resented it.

So she called Michelle, her best friend. They'd worked together, partied together. Yes the baby had meant they hadn't seen each other as much over the past year, but Eleanor could depend on Michelle. She wasn't just level headed she was also the brightest person Eleanor knew. If anyone could tell her what Rose needed, it would be Michelle.

Straight to answerphone. Fuck! Still Michelle only lived a few blocks away. The car ride might calm Rose and with the window open a crack her fever might abate a little. It was settled. Rose struggled listlessly as Eleanor zipped a jacket over her onesie then they were in the car, Rose buckled into her seat, and on their way.

The living room light was on. Michelle was home, thank god. With the baby nestled against her chest Eleanor rang the doorbell. She waited for what seemed like forever as the heat of Rose's forehead scorched her throat. No answer.

She glanced around at the parked cars. Michelle's was there. She must be home. An icy chill doused her face as she saw another, all too familiar, car. She shrugged. It was a popular model and a common colour. It didn't mean anything.

Even so, as she moved toward the living room window, her breathing grew ragged and her heart pounded nervously. No, she was being silly. It only looked like Chris' car.

Through a gap in the curtains she surveyed the living room. Champagne and glasses. Discarded clothes. Chris' briefcase. *Oh fuck no!*

She ran back to the door and pressed the doorbell. She held it down, shaking with anger. Three evenings last week, four the week before. Work had been hectic. He was needed in the office. She was unreasonable to expect him to let his colleagues down so she might bathe in peace. A window opened above and the flushed face of her friend peered out. Her friend.

Eleanor shook her head and ran for the car. Michelle called her name.

'Wait. It isn't what you think. He ... Oh Eleanor wait please. I'm your friend.'

Feet thundered down the stairs as Eleanor lay the still sleeping infant on the carseat and hurried to the driver's door. The car was locked and the engine started as two people ran into the street from Michelle's house, dressed in robes that fluttered like vultures' wings around their bare legs.

She floored the accelerator pedal and took off.

That had been three weeks ago. Chris hadn't stepped foot inside the house since then.

The garbage truck had left the street and the room returned to near silence. Only the white noise of the monitor was audible. Eleanor wiped tears from her eyes. How long since she had slept in her own bed? Eyelids, heavy like steel shutters. Damp lashes clung to each other. Her shoulders relaxed into sleep.

A wooshing sound hurtled past her head from behind the sofa. Her left ear exploded in pain. Awake she touched the ragged flesh gently. The stitches hadn't dissolved yet. The wound was still new. Too fresh to heal. Especially as she kept prodding it, like she had prodded Rose's motionless body ...

They were in the car. Eleanor's only thought was to get away. At the junction she braked too late and too hard. Something shot forward, past her head, catching the edge of her earlobe. The windscreen exploded outwards. A white shape hurtled ahead. It flew across the street before it plummeted, bounced and came to rest in the gutter.

Eleanor touched her bleeding ear and peered over her shoulder to the back seat. The baby seat was empty. The straps loose.

Sweating, Eleanor unbuckled her seatbelt and opened the car door. The white bundle remained where it had landed moments before. Unable to tear her eyes away she crossed the intersection. Behind her she heard voices getting closer, louder. She recognised them but didn't look away from the shape that would haunt every single moment of sleep until the day she checked out from life with a bottle of pills and a hot bath.

She prodded the padded velour bundle with her fingertip and gasped as a glass shard buried itself into her flesh. There was a crowd now. People gathered in a circle. Someone touched her shoulder. Someone screamed, maybe it was her. They pulled her away. She saw her car again. No scratch on the paintwork. Only the shattered windscreen reminded her what had happened.

'Where's Rose?' she asked.

Michelle wrapped her in her arms, but she stank of Chris' sweat and Eleanor pulled away.

'Where's my baby?'

Chris bent down towards the bundle. A few hushed voices asked him not to touch anything. He picked the white shape up and rocked it. Tears poured from his eyes.

'You killed her,' he growled. 'You fucking bitch. You murdered Rose.'

The Changeling
TW: Self harm

'I'm glad I came,' Miranda shouts into Evelyn's ear.

Her ear is pierced with a multitude of silver-coloured studs and rings. Evelyn smiles warmly, her berry-coloured lips closed. 'Welcome to *The Crypt*,' she breathes as the track finishes.

Less than a week ago, Miranda posted a message on an alternative online forum.

'Hi, I'm new to the Goth scene and need some advice. I don't have any Gothic friends and I'm too shy to speak to the people I see on the street. Where does everyone hang out? Who can I ask to go to a club with me? I really love the music but I'm still learning about clothes and stuff. Help me. Miranda.'

Evelyn's reply was almost instant. 'Hi Miranda. If you want, we can meet at *The Crypt* this Saturday. I'll recognise you from your profile photo, so just come along any time after ten. Evelyn. P.S. I've added a link to the club info.'

Miranda cannot see Evelyn in the swarm of black-wrapped

bodies, pierced faces, pale skin and back-combed hair. She clutches a crumpled profile photo, but it is useless. The club is a tribe to which she does not belong. The air invades her nose with scents of talc and sweat. Teeth glow, as do the white and neon flyers on every table. Drinks shine like lanterns. She feels disorientated as she pushes past damp bodies, apologising, searching.

The lightest touch on her shoulder is Evelyn's introduction. She smiles and grabs Miranda's hand, pulling her into the crowd.

'I love this song,' Evelyn announces.

The pulse of the music is fast. Bodies rise and fall around them. Evelyn's arms frame her face; her breasts and shoulders stab at the air in time with the beat of the music. Her huge boots seem weightless as she bounces.

Moving her body self-consciously, Miranda feels envious of her companion's grace. The track changes and the music slows. Miranda manages a more natural movement, swaying her body like a cobra, losing herself in the dance. Evelyn smiles at her in approval then takes Miranda's hand and leads her to the bar.

'Vodka and Coke,' Evelyn says to the tattooed barman. He nods and mixes her drink. 'You?'

'Vodka and Coke sounds good.' Miranda has never tasted vodka before.

Drinks drunk, they rush back to the dance-floor. The

music is everything; it fills the air; it fills the dancers' bodies; it dissolves time. Miranda feels like a dark Cinderella when the club's lights come on at the end of the night. Exotic bodies, which had once confused and frightened her, shrink away embarrassed in the harsh light, until only a few drunks remain. Miranda follows Evelyn to the coat check, feeling torn - wanting to stay, to dance until dawn, but worrying about the time.

'Mum's gonna kill me,' she says, too loudly. 'I've never been out this late before.'

'Come to my place,' Evelyn whispers. 'We can listen to music and talk. You can face your mum in the morning.'

Evelyn's bedsit is a short walk from the night club. The room is small and dark with a strange, but not unpleasant, smell. Evelyn takes off her velvet coat and helps Miranda out of her jacket. She drapes both over a chair and crouches down to switch on her music player. A guitar intro leads into deep, incomprehensible vocals and the sound of violins.

'Who's this?' Miranda asks.

'Lacrimosa - they're German. Do you like?'

'It's beautiful.'

'Here, drink this.' Evelyn hands Miranda a cloudy green drink.

Miranda reaches for the glass and takes a sip. It tastes of aniseed and, beneath that, a hint of something earthy. The music relaxes her. Her face prickles with the heat. She stares at her new friend, but finds that she can't focus on Evelyn's face. The room is melting; everything shifts and changes, like being under water without the fear of drowning.

Evelyn's black hair moves. Her mouth twists. Her face alternates between beautiful and grotesque. There is a strange glow in her green eyes. 'I want you. I want to be you.'

'I love you,' Miranda replies.

In her peripheral vision she sees a flash of metal as Evelyn cuts Miranda's forearm with a razor blade. The pain rouses her and she tries to stand up, but she has forgotten how to tell her muscles to move. Like gelatine, she sinks into the old velvet couch. Everything feels wrong. She tries to say *no*, shake her head, anything.

Evelyn sucks at the small wound. She drinks, licking the puncture and surrounding skin, like a French kiss but more intimate. Miranda's fear turns to desire which spreads from between her legs, to her stomach and up. As the feeling reaches her throat she floats upwards. From the ceiling, she gazes at the raven-haired lover crouched over her vacated body. Parts of Evelyn vanish, like broken pixels on a computer screen. Her solidity changes into a mist which focuses on the thread of blood across Miranda's arm, pushing into the wound, then Evelyn and the mist are gone and Miranda is alone, then nothing.

Miranda wakes up in Evelyn's room. The music is still playing. She clasps her head between her hands as pain blinds her; forcing her to sit, eyes clamped shut, head in hands, until the agony fades.

Daylight pierces the velvet curtains. Miranda body protests against every movement as she rises unsteadily to her feet.

'Evelyn?'

There is no answer. Walking into the kitchenette, Miranda sees a bottle of bright green liquid on the otherwise empty counter. The refrigerator is empty too. Tearing through the kitchen, throwing open cupboard door after cupboard door, she finds nothing. She searches frantically for anything that might belong to Evelyn: clothes, computer, letters. There is nothing except her discarded velvet coat. Miranda grabs her bag and Evelyn's coat from the chair. Shrugging into it, she leaves the flat and hobbles to the bus stop, one hand shielding her eyes from the sun.

Her mother shouts as Miranda opens her front door. 'Where in hell have you been, Miranda? I've been worried sick. I phoned the police. Why didn't you come home? Why didn't you call? What were you thinking? Have you been drinking?'

She grabs Miranda's shoulders, but the girl shakes her off and pushes past. Miranda walks upstairs in silence, leaving her mother's demands for explanations hanging in the air.

That evening she returns to Evelyn's bedsit. Getting into the building is easy. She enters as someone leaves. They hardly notice her. When she reaches Evelyn's door, she knocks. The door swings open, revealing a dark room. She waits at the threshold, allowing her eyes to adjust. She notices a shape in the far corner of the otherwise empty room. She hears crying and smells wet grass and musk. Her hand flails across the wall but she cannot find a light switch. Keeping the door open, she steps towards the shape. The sobbing grows louder.

'Evelyn?'

The crying stops. Miranda's blood rushes through her, roaring in her ears. Reaching out toward the squat shape, she hears a low growl and withdraws in fear. She tilts her head, trying to understand the blackness before it pounces and a shock of icy air makes her stumble backwards. A large dog cuts through the darkness and out of the room.

Miranda sits on the floor, gasping for breath. The carpet feels sticky beneath her hands. Black algae coat her fingers. She springs up, repulsed, and runs from the apartment.

Her hand itches, a burning sensation that spreads up her arm to the raised red line. She scratches it, but the irritation is deeper than she can reach.

The next few weeks are spent avoiding her mother's criticisms. 'The school phoned. Where were you today, Miranda? You can't spend your days in bed. You have responsibilities too, Miranda. Stop scratching, have you caught lice? Miranda … Miranda! Are you even listening to me?'

She tries not to listen, hiding in her bedroom, plugged into her iPod. She dyes her hair black, and in the process the bathroom tiles, shower rose and two bath towels. She attempts to rub the stains off the tiles, but throws the towels away.

She pierces herself. Ears first, then nose and bottom lip. She uses a needle. At the moment the metal pierces Miranda's skin, she is back in Evelyn's room, feeling the bite of the razor blade once again. She welcomes this penetration into herself, the burning of cold metal. Gathering drops of blood on the tips of her fingers, she sucks them. The way her ears jangle when she moves, it is like music. It is her music.

Miranda becomes a regular at *The Crypt*. Every second Saturday she goes, hoping to see Evelyn again. She dances to the music and drinks too heavily, but the evenings seem hollow. She searches the internet, spending hours on forums and chat-rooms, hunting for anyone who might have seen Evelyn. One guy sends Miranda a message telling her he's Evelyn's brother. She meets him near *The Crypt*. His bare arms are covered in tiny cuts and his eyes shine.

'Come with me. I'll take you to her.'

Miranda is tempted to believe his words; to go with him. But when he tries to urge her into a car, she runs away, afraid he is lying.

One night, at *The Crypt*, she spots Evelyn across the dance floor, but when she reaches the spot Evelyn has gone. Miranda spins around, searching for her friend. Each face is unique to her. The confused mass of black has taken on diversity with familiarity. She recognises many of the faces: people she has danced with, drunk with, seduced, people who have given her cigarettes, alcohol, speed, coke, but Evelyn isn't among them.

She spots a red-haired girl in a *Ruby Gloom* t-shirt and baggy blue jeans who appears lost and out of place. Miranda approaches her and touches her shoulder, lightly. 'Are you okay?'

'I'm looking for Evelyn.' The red-head sounds frightened and confused. 'Do you know where she is?'

Miranda smiles warmly, her berry-coloured lips closed. 'You've found her,' she reassures the girl. 'Wanna dance?'

Demons are a Girl's Best Friend

It was on the day her mother died that Natalie began seeing demons.

"I'm sorry," Doctor Wills said, and his face did look sorry. Sympathy was his default expression. How many times had he repeated the same words to people like her? "All we can do is make her comfortable now."

Natalie nodded, unable to form sentences. The letters were in her head, but they were jumbled like jigsaw pieces, and she was certain some were missing.

"Maybe you should let your brothers and sisters know, if they want to see her before … Is there anyone I can call to sit with you? I know it's a shock. She seemed to be improving."

Was he taking the unformed words directly from her brain? She only realised what she wanted to say after the doctor provided the answer. Or was it experience? Did everyone ask the same questions when they knew that soon a loved one would leave them?

He made her feel much younger than her thirty-five years.

She shook her head. No one would come to share her

burden. Natalie would summon her brothers and sisters back to their painful past, but they would arrive too late to help. Instead they would pull up to the front door in their huge cars and rush to the room that smelled of wilting flowers. She supposed she should get fresh ones. They'd forget Natalie was there. Forget she was anything more than a messenger, the bringer of sad news. They would be nursing their own grief, and would have no space to share hers. The burden of the middle child. Forgotten. Ignored.

"Please call me if anything changes," Doctor Wills said before he left.

What could change? Hadn't he said this was it? They could only make her comfortable and wait for her to die. Natalie's mother.

Natalie sat by the bed and held her mother's limp hand. She didn't squeeze, but rather cradled the claw of loose flesh over brittle bone. The illness had taken everything, but the doctors couldn't even give it a name. At least Mother was at home now. Unconscious in her own bed. The doctor's powerlessness had given her that at least.

Her mother grumbled in her sleep. A bad dream? Or had she heard the doctor's words? Did she know she was dying?

Natalie should call her siblings. They would expect her to, but they expected too much. Where were they when diapers had to be changed? Where were they when vomit soaked sheets needed to be washed? They had their careers – newsreader, beautician, lawyer and accountant. There wasn't room in their lives to nurse their sick mother. That fell to Natalie, the under-achiever. Forgotten. Ignored.

She pulled a wet sponge from a bowl that was the last remaining piece of a wedding set before the matching plates and dishes had been smashed in rage. She squeezed out the excess, the tears she couldn't cry, and gently wiped her mother's brow. A dribble of dark liquid ran down the sick woman's chin. The grumbling ceased and Mother was calm again.

Natalie would call them, but before they arrived and pushed her aside she would spend time alone, with Mother, chasing away the demons that plagued her fevered sleep.

"I came as fast as I could. I had to cancel an appointment with an important client. Am I too late?" That was Stephen's greeting. No, 'how are you', no, 'I'm sorry'; just an 'am I too late'. Did half of him hope he was? That he wouldn't have to linger in that old house for too long?

"She's upstairs, sleeping," Natalie replied, taking the coat that he seemed unable to hang for himself. "You're the first to arrive."

He snorted.

"Do you want some tea?" she asked.

He nodded and mounted the first step. "I'll be up …

there." He stared at Natalie for a moment, and she wondered what he wanted to say. But he must have decided against speaking. A moment later he turned his back to her again and climbed.

When Natalie brought the tea, Stephen was sitting in a chair, a few feet from the bed, watching the rise and fall of their mother's chest.

"Did the doctor say how long?" he asked, taking the cup and saucer from Natalie.

"I don't think he knows, but soon."

The doorbell rang and Natalie hurried away.

Natalie cooked dinner for them all. Perhaps fear or grief robbed them of their sense of taste, because none of them seemed to enjoy the food, even though it was a dish their mother used to make.

They talked around Natalie, discussing their various careers, their important clients, ignoring the elephant in the upstairs room, while catching up with self-congratulatory anecdotes. Natalie realised how much she hated every one of them.

"Is she ever awake?" Sophie asked.

Sophie's manicured nail dragged along Natalie's index finger as she took a cup of coffee from her sister the following morning. It didn't hurt Natalie's hand, but it grazed her heart as did the words. What had Sophie expected? A jolly family get together?

"Sometimes," Natalie answered. "But not often and never for long. Not for a month now."

"And there's nothing they can do?"

"Only make her comfortable."

"It's just … I have to get back. Do you think she knows I came?"

Natalie shrugged, biting back the vicious words she wanted to scream.

"I mean if she doesn't know I'm here …"

"Do you know I'm here?" Natalie asked.

Her sister looked at her askew. "Of course I do. You were always so close to her. I'm sure she appreciates it. We all do."

Well that's okay then, Natalie thought furiously, *as long as you can say you appreciate me, what more can I expect? Maybe you should all just fuck off and leave me to it then.*

Their mother died two hours after Sophie had driven away in her vintage Mercedes Benz. Stephen made the call to their absentee sister.

The death wasn't dramatic. One moment Mother's chest rose and fell and then it didn't rise again. For a long while they watched, all four of them – Stephen, Charles,

Madeline and Natalie. It seemed like a held breath, but it was held too long.

Charles spoke first. "I think she's gone."

Stephen and Madeline nodded in eager agreement. A collective sigh was exhaled. It was over. They could get back to their respective lives.

To be certain, Charles checked her pulse.

"I'll call Doctor Wills," Charles said, fishing his phone from his jacket pocket. "Do you have his number?"

"I'll call Sophie," Stephen said.

Natalie sat, registering the flustered movements of her siblings in her periphery vision. She focused on her mother's face. There was a trace of a smile. Was Mother as relieved it was over as her brothers and sister seemed to be?

When Natalie glanced towards her siblings she saw their eyes flash red. Their features creased up into sharp grey and khaki lines below their eyes. A moment later their taut flesh softened and their normal skin tones were restored. She assumed it was her grief that caused the strange transformations, or theirs.

"Doctor Wills' number?" Charles asked again.

They took her away in a white van. Natalie's mother. Natalie wondered what she might do now.

The others huddled together in the sitting room, bent like crones towards a central point she couldn't see. She decided to make tea for everyone, but even the kettle looked different. The water wouldn't fall in right. It splashed her hand instead. The scene melted. She realised she was crying.

"Are you okay?" Madeline asked.

When had Madeline sneaked in behind her? How long had Natalie been bent over the sink, weeping?

Natalie rubbed her eyes. She straightened her back and turned to her sister, but Madeline wasn't there. It was strange that this thing used Madeline's voice. It might have tricked Natalie if her eyes weren't clear and dry. But this thing, touching Natalie's arm, was not her oldest sister, the beloved newsreader on national television. Not the special princess that their father used to call her. Not the smart one like their aunt Lucy used to say. Not the pretty one, as their mother had often crooned. This creature was not pretty, it was grotesque. Green and grey flesh hung in folds around its flame-red eyes. The strands of hair that clung to its scalp were knotted and matted like a nest of snakes. Its sharp teeth were black when it attempted a friendly smile. It was the disease. The demon that had haunted Mother's dreams and sucked her life slowly away. Natalie had to kill it. She had to avenge her mother's death and save herself. Thankfully there was a knife on the draining board. She only had to reach it before the demon sensed it had been discovered.

She curled her fingers around the handle. The demon seemed oblivious to her plans. Its soothing voice tried to console her, like an older sibling was supposed to do. Then the demon fled and Madeline stood there. The folded skin was replaced by crimson rings around tired eyes.

"Is it you?" Natalie asked, dropping the knife with a loud clatter.

Madeline's mouth formed an O. She reached across the breach and drew Natalie into an embrace. A few moments later, Natalie found she'd been marched to the living room where her younger brothers sat.

"Charles, can you call Doctor Wills again, please? I'm worried about Nat."

Doctor Wills gave her pills. He told her it was her nerves, but his long nose looked like a plague mask and his black jacket like raven's wings. Natalie knew she couldn't trust him. He'd let her mother die.

"One of us should stay," Madeline said, looking pointedly at the others. Obviously it couldn't be her.

"Maybe she should come with one of us," Sophie suggested. She'd returned at last, only wanting to leave again as quickly as possible. "A change of scene might be what she needs. This house is ..."

"I'm not leaving," Natalie said. "This is my home."

Charles, the fourth child, the first son, the lawyer, piped in. "Nat, you know we're going to sell the house, don't you?"

His eyes flashed red as the demon surfaced. He made his living sucking from the marrow from all that was good, and now he expected financial gain from his own mother's death. How could he? Mother's mattress was still warm. She who had struggled to birth him for two days in agonizing labour. Natalie had only been three when Charles tore his way out from their precious parent, but she remembered the pallor that remained in Mother's skin for weeks after she came home. She remembered helping her older sisters to take care of the screaming parasite while her mother rested. Her sisters must remember too. Charles was a selfish brat. He always had been, and yet he was the favourite, the prince. His birth put an abrupt end to Natalie's childhood, and her life-long job as a caregiver began. Now he planned to kick her out of her home for a measly payout?

"Demon!" she screamed.

"Where are those pills?" Madeline asked. "Have you taken any yet? Nat?"

"This is ridiculous," Stephen said, the accountant, the pragmatist. "She needs care, professional care. It's a breakdown. We left Nat here with Mum. We should pay for her care. She just needs to rest."

They stood above her, wringing their hands and working their jaws, thinking on the one hand of the holidays and cars they'd buy when the house was sold, and on the other how they'd let their sister take the burden they should have shared equally. They owed her something, not too much of course, but something. Something that would help them sleep at night without guilt-ridden dreams. They said none of this out loud but, in their twisted faces, Natalie saw the truth.

"A breakdown?" Madeline asked, studying the bottle of pills. "Is that what these are for? I just thought she needed a sedative."

"How can a doctor justify leaving her here with us and a bottle of anti-psychotics?" Sophie said. "It isn't right."

"It's been a long day," Charles said. "Let's get Nat into bed, then we can talk."

One of the demonic siblings, Natalie couldn't tell them apart now, tucked her into bed. Its breath, as it said goodnight, smelled like a puff of putrid air escaping an ancient tomb. The narrow lips barely concealed its shark-like teeth. It shut the door behind it when it left, but she wasn't left alone. A terrifying face lurked in every corner of the room, plus the one above her who kept guard. She couldn't move, and she couldn't sleep. Her jaw ached, but she couldn't close her mouth. The demon wriggled against the ceiling. Its eyes never left her face. It didn't even blink. She tried not to blink either, but her eyeballs were burning, her skin too. She pulled the covers over her head and closed her eyes, praying that her dead mother was there to protect her.

She slept, albeit fitfully, and when Natalie awoke and the rays of morning sunlight which poured through the window cleansed her room. The demons were gone. Her siblings were gone too. They must have left in the night, while the demons trapped her in bed. None of their cars were outside and none of their beds had been slept in. For a moment Natalie wondered whether she'd dreamed it all, but when she checked her mother's bed it too was empty. Empty and cold.

As she filled the kettle to make tea, the sound of water drumming against metal calmed her. There was a note left on the kitchen table. She ignored it. Whatever the demons wanted to tell her could wait.

The phone rang. Natalie felt a lump in her throat. It would be someone for Mother. Anyone who rang to speak to Natalie used her mobile.

"Hello?"

"Good morning, I'm sorry to disturb you. Am I speaking to Miss Natalie Green?" The voice sounded formal, official. The funeral home maybe?

"Yes. Who is this?"

"I'm sorry. I'm calling from Severen and Wilde. We're your late mother's solicitors. I am sorry for your loss. I'm phoning to see if you can come into our office tomorrow at eleven, for the reading of your mother's will."

"Isn't my brother in charge of all that? I thought he'd be the executor."

"No, your mother wanted someone outside the family to handle her affairs. Are you available?"

Natalie nodded. "Sure. Eleven, right? Give me the address."

Sophie studied her nails while the others studied the menu. Natalie tried to hide her smirk. It served them all right. They could moan and groan, but their mother had left the house to Natalie and there was nothing they could do about it.

Madeline eschewed food in favour of green tea. She claimed she wasn't hungry. Natalie was sure she heard her sister's stomach rumble in protest.

After lunch they would head to the funeral parlour together to discuss arrangements. By three Natalie would be alone again. She didn't mind too much. She had expected their desertion, but she was surprised the subject of her mental health had been dropped so quickly, unless it was a subject they planned to discuss in her absence.

The coffin seemed extravagant for an object that was to be burned. Natalie suspected it was a final fuck you to a community who had pitied their mother rather than respecting her. The town had considered their family too large, too disruptive, full of wayward children and a deadbeat dad. They thought she'd married beneath her, and had never expected four of the five children to grow up successful and rich.

It was very different to the ceremony they'd held for their father a decade before. That was a quiet affair and only their mother had cried. The flames that ate their dad's remains were no doubt aided by the alcohol in his blood, or so they'd joked when out earshot of their mother. For some reason their mother had loved him. For many reasons the children didn't. Perhaps if he'd lived longer he would have found a way to crush all their dreams.

But Mother was different. Mother was loved, by her children and the wider community. The chapel was full and voices rose in song to wish her safe travels.

At the wake, Doctor Wills approached Natalie. She was busy making tea in the kitchen. She realised that making tea had become her default setting, but it felt healthier than the alternative. It calmed her and made her feel useful, while allowing her time away from the streams of conversations that echoed around both reception rooms.

"How are you, Natalie?" he asked.

"Much better, doctor. Thank you for coming," she replied.

She avoided looking at him. His hawkish nose was all she saw when she focused on his face.

"Do you need more pills?" he asked.

"No thank you."

"Can you come in for a check up next week?" he urged.

"I'll try," she replied, hoping to dismiss him.

It worked and with a long sigh he left her to it. She wondered which of her brothers or sisters had urged him to see her, and whether they'd been motivated by worry or avarice.

The demons kept Natalie company. Sometimes they brushed across the faces of people she met, momentarily changing their features, and at others they crouched in her bedroom waiting for nightfall when they could follow her into her dreams. She wondered whether she growled as she slept, like her mother, but there was no one to ask.

When she asked the demons what they wanted they were reticent. When she persisted with her interrogation they flitted away, but they always returned, normally when she was too tired to argue.

They spoke to her of other things. They were her advisers. They warned her to keep the house clean and tidy. They made her flush away the pills. They told her that her siblings were watching, waiting for her to fail so they could sell the house and lock her up.

They let her know when the doctor was about to knock on her door, so she could hide and pretend to be out.

They painted beautiful pictures in her imagination of far off places full of vibrant hues that shimmered when she focused on them. They reminded her to shower, and bustled her out of the door each morning, telling her that healthy minds needed friends.

She began to see beauty in their creased flesh and ruby eyes, convinced that her mother had sent them to take care of her solitary daughter. She looked forward to night when they would play with her in her dreams.

She grew stronger. Less afraid of the judgements of others. Less in awe of her siblings.

She got a job. With her experience and two weeks of basic induction, she landed a position with an agency, working in community care. It was comfortably familiar. Something she was good at, taking care of the elderly and infirm. Her clients' demons swelled Natalie's retinue of friends. She gathered them to her bosom and accepted them. Sometimes they'd follow her home.

When Natalie was sad, demons stroked her hair. When she was angry, they smashed things. When she wanted affection, they caressed her skin. In return they were grateful to be seen and understood.

Fewer people called at the house. Outside, people smiled at her, but she always saw a sliver of fear in their eyes. Inside, she knew she was loved.

The demons taught her things, ancient languages,

forgotten songs and poignant tales. They opened her eyes to her own beauty, no longer overshadowed by her older sisters, but fresh and bright. They encouraged her to take risks, experiment with make-up, dye her hair, wear more revealing clothes. The smiles of the outside world became hungry leers. The sliver of fear changed to envy. The jealousy and desire of other people changed how she saw herself, and her confidence grew.

A year, almost to the day, after her mother died, Natalie awoke to the sharp sound of shattering glass.

"Someone's inside the house," the demons warned her.

"Three men," they confirmed.

"It's okay. Go downstairs and confront them. We'll protect you," they promised.

She trusted the voices, but still felt afraid. She wrapped a dressing gown around herself and opened the bedroom door, silently. She listened. The demons were right. She heard voices and footsteps on the floor below. She considered calling the police, but knew they'd arrive too late to help. But the demons had promised their protection. She overcame the desire to hide and stepped lightly onto the landing.

Natalie crept down the stairs, avoiding the ones that creaked. Three men, that's what the demons had said. Instead she saw teenagers, so young they were more like children, gathered in the sitting room. They'd removed her grandmother's portrait from the wall and were staring at the safe. The closest one to Natalie shivered.

"Why's it so cold," he whispered.

Natalie smiled. She was warm enough. It must be the demons, messing with him.

"Read those numbers again," the one closest to the safe said. He kept his voice low.

"Twenty-three, sixty-seven, forty-nine."

The one at the safe tried the dial again. "No. She must have changed the combination. Who wants to wake her?"

Natalie slipped back into the shadows of the hallway and watched as one boy reluctantly climbed the stairs.

"Your brother?" one of the demons asked.

Natalie shook her head. No, her family wouldn't send people to rob her. That was insane.

She heard each of the doors being opened upstairs, then hurried footsteps descending. The boy returned to the others without glancing Natalie's way.

"Empty," he told them, no longer bothering to whisper. "But one of the beds's been slept in."

"Search the house," the leader, 'safe boy' said. "I'll work on getting this open."

Natalie fled to the kitchen. She grabbed the same knife she'd once raised against her sister, and crouched behind a cabinet.

One boy followed another into the kitchen, perhaps they'd heard the clatter of the cutlery drawer. One made eye contact with Natalie and shivered again. He was wide eyed with messy light brown hair, a Dickensian street cherub. He pointed in her direction but didn't move towards her.

"There," he said.

The other took three steps then stopped in his tracks. This one was less pretty, but no less scared. Natalie didn't need to ask the intruders what was wrong. She knew why they were afraid. She felt the demons surrounding her, bristling with anger, and knew the boys sensed them too.

With a shrug of her shoulders she was pushed from her body. Natalie dangled in the corner of the kitchen ceiling, as small and unnoticeable as a spider. She watched the boys shake with terror, and saw the object of their fear just as clearly. Natalie's flesh moved from behind the cupboard without any conscious effort of her will.

As her body rose to its feet, the two boys inhaled. As it spread her arms, they turned to run. Her hair moved around the serene face as though she was under water. Her dressing gown undulated too. The current puppet master of her flesh wasn't concerned about her modesty. It laughed, this body that was once her own, and with the air expelled from her lungs the demons stormed ahead.

She watched in horror, powerless. The cowering teens were children. But the demons didn't care.

"Nasty vermin invading our lair," one roared.

"Disrespecting us. Breaking in to steal what isn't theirs."

"No reaction would be an overreaction."

"Our fury is justified. Our anger is righteous. Natalie will be avenged."

They were rage, and Natalie's body was at the centre of it all. Without her interference, she was all powerful. The horror and powerlessness she'd felt at first, watching from above, changed to awe and acceptance. The boys' fear gave her power, and she revelled in it. The moment she felt the rightness of her body's actions she was reabsorbed by her flesh.

One boy screamed as he was lifted then thrown at the wall. Natalie heard bones crack. Blood dribbled from his lips as his crumpled body fell to the floor.

She turned to the other. His eyes were even bigger now and wet with tears. He was the sensitive one, the one who had shivered when her demons had touched him. He saw them all, every pulsing molecule, and his mind cracked.

"Who sent you?" she asked.

His slack jaw couldn't form a reply. Bubbles of saliva popped around his trembling lips. His pupils expanded to fill his eyes. She saw her reflection in them. She was terrifying.

She abandoned him and made her way to the sitting room.

"Who sent you?" she asked.

The boy jumped and removed his earplugs. He looked embarrassed when he faced her rather than afraid. As if a teacher had caught him misbehaving in class.

"Who gave you the number?" she tried again.

He looked behind her and saw he was alone. He shrugged. "Sorry, love, nothing personal. Just a man in a pub."

"What did he look like?"

"Blond hair, kind of ugly, bad skin."

The description didn't fit either of her brothers. Maybe they'd hired someone else to do their dirty work, or maybe she'd been right and this wasn't her family. But who else would have the number her mother had used for the family safe?

"My mates, okay?" he asked.

She shrugged. "So you need the new number, huh?"

He didn't know how to reply. He struggled to focus on her face.

"I'm sorry. We'll just go," he said, but didn't move a muscle.

"Just ask me," she said.

"Huh?"

"For the safe number. Just ask me."

His brow furrowed as if he'd forgotten his lines and needed Natalie to prompt him.

"Ask me!" she yelled.

"Umm, what's the combination?" he asked.

"Six, six and fucking six." She laughed. "Get it?"

He trembled, but didn't turn back to the safe. He stared at her while sweat dripped from his forehead and over his cheeks. His fear was delicious.

She let out a scream that forced the boy backwards and pinned him to the wall. She took a step towards him. He tried to make himself small by sinking to the floor. A greasy black smear stained the wallpaper. It had a head and arms. Natalie wondered whether his shadow self had entered the wall.

With his cocky confidence gone, safe boy looked younger still. For a moment Natalie hesitated. These children were no threat to her. She should let them go. They would not return, neither would their story, should they choose to share it, be believed.

The demons wanted to finish it now. Kill the kids, dispose of their bodies. Their venom shook Natalie, it frightened her. She'd been relying on their good counsel for twelve months. They'd kept her loneliness at bay. They'd made sure she ate, cleaned, slept and woke up again. Defying them, after they'd taken care of her, felt wrong, but so did killing the boys. It was messed up. She hadn't asked for any of this. But she wasn't sure she could make the demons leave, even if she wanted to. She belonged to the voices, her demons. They'd adopted her after her mother had died and she had thought Mother sent them to protect her. But now, she began to doubt this logic. What if they had been her mother's illness? What if they had left her mother's shell after she drew her last breath to join with Natalie. What if they were slowly killing her as they'd killed her mother, day by day, hour by hour. She felt stronger now, but she was less herself than a portal for the voices. A vessel to carry them around.

"Go now, and take your friends with you," she yelled.

The boy darted away. She saw gratitude and relief in his nervous smile. She had beaten the demons back, but for how long, and what would they do to Natalie when she was alone?

Natalie couldn't remember falling asleep, but the sitting room was bright with sunlight when she opened her eyes. She replaced the portrait of her grandmother, hiding the safe. She stared for a while at the silhouette safe boy had left behind and hoped it would fade. She moved a lamp in front of it to hide the stain. Order had been restored.

The kitchen would take a lot more effort to put right. A table had been upturned and blood spatter marked the spot where the first boy fell. He wasn't here, which meant he was alive at least, or had been when safe boy had taken him.

Wind howled through a smashed pane in the back

door.

"Look what you've done," Natalie chastised the demons.

When she received no reply she felt both relieved and sad. The voices had been terrifying, but they were her only companions. She didn't know whether she'd survive without them. She told herself they were still there but sulking. This silent treatment was her punishment for spoiling their fun. They'd forgive her eventually.

She considered phoning the police, but knew she couldn't explain what they'd find. She wondered whether she should call her brothers and sisters, but they'd been campaigning to find her mentally unfit and would use it as an excuse to evict her from the house. The only option was to clean it up herself. It was obvious the demons didn't intend to help.

"Where are you?" she asked. Only the wind replied.

The glazier wanted her to inform the police. "If you've had a break in, or attempted break in, your insurance will cover it."

She thanked him, but paid in cash.

The house felt too big. She rattled around inside it. Its empty rooms echoed her hollow existence.

She called the demons again, but they were still ignoring her.

Weeks passed, then months. Natalie cared for the old and infirm, but she no longer encountered their demons. Her clients seemed like shadows, as if their vibrancy had been a symptom of demonic possession? Natalie was losing her will to endure. She didn't eat. She woke up in front of the television, having forgotten to go to her bed. Even incontinent old women remarked on her pungent smell.

When she lost her job she didn't have the energy to care.

It was then Natalie's family descended. Their sympathetic smiles did little to hide their glee at her demise. They'd expected this, but thought it would happen sooner. Natalie couldn't take care of herself. She needed to be looked after. The house was divided equally between the four siblings and Natalie was sent away.

"I miss them," Natalie said.

The therapist's room was warm. The low lighting seemed to dance on the walls. The couch was soft. Her body sank into it.

"Your family?" the therapist asked.

"My demons. I should have let them kill those boys."

The therapist scribbled something in her notes. Natalie closed her eyes and smiled. At least she wasn't alone.

Dance the Ghost With Me
TW: Male on male violent assault

Simon stood up. The room spun. How long had he been unconscious? The bathroom came into focus around him. Someone was gagging behind one of the stall doors. Memories of an attack rushed into his mind, but he felt no pain. Maybe it was a distant memory or the pain receptors in his brain had been dulled by alcohol. The snarling mouth, the rank breath, the glint of metal, all of it kept replaying in front of him, but it was an illusion, the ghost of a memory.

Where was he? The layout of the room seemed familiar, but the décor was all wrong. A well-loved mural of The Scream had been painted over in dull dove grey, to be replaced by descriptions of sexual practises and telephone numbers scribbled in black and red Sharpies. The floor was different too. The old black and white vinyl had been replaced at some point by an even scruffier pitted grey with red speckles. Was it blood? No, too regular to be blood, a pattern on the floor covering, nothing more sinister. Although that was sinister enough in this familiar yet unfamiliar room that made Simon's head spin.

He approached a mirror, bolted to the wall, above a

sink that was overflowing with plastic pint glasses. He saw the graffitied wall reversed, shielding his eyes from a painfully bright halogen strip light that bounced back into the room in all directions from a convex panel that framed the glass. But where was his face?

A door creaked and a figure shuffled into view. Dark hair, tanned skin and hedgehog like designer stubble above a black short-sleeved shirt, the top few buttons open. Simon's body shook so violently he thought his skeleton might shatter. This was not his face. He mentally catalogued the differences. He was cleanly shaven, his hair much longer and darker, his nose and bottom lip pierced with silver rings. His skin was paler, perpetually hidden from the sun. The colour of the shirt was right, but he would never wear that style. It was nightmarish, that green-gilled face, that faux-male-model look, the heavy eyelids and strong jawline. He put his hand to his chin, no stubble, piercing still in place. The face in the mirror bowed for a moment before retreating. As the door opened, the rush of adrenaline-fuelled electronic dance music from the club swallowed Simon in one greedy gulp. Was this hell?

He was squatting on a faux-marble surface between two of the three sinks when the door opened again. His buckled winklepicker boots were tucked under his black denim shrouded thighs, like The Crow, balancing on a rooftop, as he watched silverfish scuttle along the skirting boards and under discarded sheets of toilet paper, some of which had obviously been used. A different face entered this time, but it was no more familiar to him than the first. This one had a more established beard that almost but not entirely obscured the acne scars on his cheeks. Simon watched as the man relieved himself into the urinal trough and left again. Limbo, not hell, Simon thought.

Faces came and faces went. With each arrival and departure the painfully upbeat music boxed Simon's ears. It created an impenetrable wall of sound that Simon could not bear to breach and so he stayed, in the relative peace of the bathroom, wondering when it would end.

He scaled the plywood walls of the toilet stalls and crouched with his back pushed against the sticky ceiling tiles. Using the bathroom as a junglegym at least altered his view for a while. From here he watched executive types snort lines of coke while avoiding stray streams of piss and chunks of projectile vomit. The image of that terrible anger returned. The thin lips drawn back over sharp teeth, a word, what was it? What was that furious mouth saying to him?

Another mouth now. This one was soft and stained purple as if smothered in blackberry juice. Lips pushed against his, then a tongue, searching inside his mouth. Sweet breath filled him. His body responded. When that memory receded, he yearned to get it back. The lips were his only comfort in this cold isolation. He wished he remembered who they belonged to.

A clenched fist and the flash of metal. Pressure then release and sticky moisture dripping down his cheek. Tears? Was he crying?

It had been hours since the last interruption of his reverie and Simon risked creeping towards the door and pulling it ajar. Silence. He opened it further and stepped out into a huge room. At the centre was a sunken dance floor. The parquet was strewn with trampled plastic and spilt liquids. Beyond it a bar, with a panel of spotlights that made the liquid inside the optics glimmer, appealingly. He needed a drink.

The room seemed empty at first. Then a shadow grew in the centre of the dance floor. Spinning and swirling, upwards and outwards. A lace skirt, a tiny waist, thick, black hair and those dark berry-coloured lips. He wanted to dance with her, this spectre. He wanted to press his lips against hers again. He knew that face. Those moist eyes that always seemed full of tears. She called herself Lucretia, like the song, and he wanted to dance with her again.

He towered over her. She was tiny, even in those impossibly high heels she wore. She kept looking past him. What did she see? Whatever it was seemed to fill her with dread. Her bottom lip trembled and he pressed his thumb gently against it. Did she smile? Did she let him through her wall of sullen silence for a moment. Now she was kissing him. Her hands wandering over his body, pulling him closer until they seemed to melt into each other for a blissful second.

'No!'

Did she say that? Perhaps, she fled from the dance floor and he started in pursuit. But as he passed the door to the bathroom he was inside it again. The Scream saw him stumble and tried to push away from the wall, but it was just as trapped as he was. Here came the snarl again, shark's eyes, foul breath and a fist wrapped tightly around a metal spike. It rushed towards him.

'Mine!'

The pressure on his eyeball was intense. The membrane, hot as fire as it stretched then popped. A rush of liquid streamed down his trembling cheek as he fell to the floor. The scream hurt his ears, he couldn't stop the noise. It filled his throat and his mind as he rocked from side to side on the floor. Still the metal pushed deeper. The snarl had morphed into an empty cave. An O shaped expression of shock and horror. The weight of a man concentrated into the head of a needle that buried deeper into his brain as electrical impulses went into overdrive then shut down and all was dark. All was nothing. Just the black hole of an open mouth and nothing.

Simon stood up. The room spun. How long had he been unconscious? The bathroom came into focus around him. Someone was gagging behind one of the stall doors. Memories of an attack rushed into his mind, but he experienced no pain. Maybe it was a distant memory or the pain receptors in his brain had been dulled by alcohol. The snarling mouth, the rank breath, the glint of metal, all of it kept replaying in front of him, but it was an illusion, the ghost of a memory ...

Cracked

Rachel studied Sam. Silhouetted against the reddening sun, he worked the bolts. Beyond him lay the twisting driveway. His excitement infected her.

'I've done it!' Sam pushed the gate open.

Rachel forced a smile and stepped through the narrow gap, hunched under her rucksack. White knuckles clutched her laptop case.

'I'll close it back up.' He replaced the bolts and shook the wire fence as if to reassure them of their protection from the outside world.

The setting sun highlighted every aspect of him: jeans pulled tight around his perfect buttocks and the narrow waist that curved fluidly between denim and the hem of his t-shirt.

'This should be fun.' She blushed and swept her eyes across pock-marked concrete.

Sam stepped towards her. His fingers closed around Rachel's and he lifted the case from her. Shoulder to shoulder they ambled along the overgrown drive of Ladyswell Asylum.

It had seemed like a great idea: their own ghost-hunter show broadcast live on Twitter, one hundred and forty characters of terror at a time. Excitement and fear battled inside Rachel from the moment she agreed to join Sam. She'd heard the ghost stories, but it was worth the risk to spend a whole night with the man of her dreams.

Seven o'clock - the shadows lengthened. They agreed to check out each abandoned building in order, to discover the best place to make camp.

The first was a two storey villa. Outside it looked like a disused school. The reinforced windows were subtly done. The hinges of the door had dropped and it stood ajar, wedged into muddy soil. They left their belongings outside to shoulder their way in. Inside, the gloom made her shudder. Her eyes fought to see a few meters ahead. Fallen rubble covered the floor. Layers of institutional-green paint peeled away from flesh-pink plaster walls. Drops of water echoed through the hall. The smell of fungi overwhelmed them.

Rachel lunged outside, gasping for fresh air. Moments later Sam followed, shaking his head. 'Too damp.'

The front door of the adjacent single-storey building was closed. The wood creaked but did not budge when Sam pushed against it with his shoulder. Rachel walked around the outside and found a side door moving in the wind.

The mesh and glass panels of the door had been smashed and torn. Spikes of broken wire stabbed the air.

Stepping inside, they crunched over broken glass and fist sized chunks of concrete. The rooms were empty, but there was no shelter or clear floor on which to rest.

Building after building was broken and unusable. As the sun dipped lower, they regretted their lack of foresight and wished they'd explored before the big night.

They reached the far corner of the "village" and an imposing two-storey building. A surgical trolley, used by vandals as a battering ram, blocked the entrance. Rachel pulled it clear and stepped inside. Sam followed close behind. The internal doors whispered their welcome as she pushed them open. Then absolute silence.

A long corridor sloped gently downwards to the left.

'This way?' Sam suggested.

Rachel nodded.

Sam shrugged and pulled a face, breaking the tension and making Rachel wheeze with laughter. They stood motionless for seconds that moved like hours, peering into the gloom.

Walking along the corridor, they realised the floor was rubble-free. On the left a glass-paned door to a small office stood open. A desk and swivel chair waited patiently, dusty but undamaged. A green filing-cabinet gaped. Files were crammed inside its drawers, case histories, lives abandoned.

'Looks good.' Sam leaned over Rachel's shoulder. His cheek almost touched hers and his voice caressed her aching ear. She swallowed hard, trying to control her shaking body.

'Why didn't they wreck this like the rest of the buildings?'

Sam shook his head. 'Dunno, but I'm glad they didn't.'

Rachel stepped forward, unpacked her laptop and switched it on. They left the computer to load up, using the time to explore. The room opposite was once a bathroom. The toilet stalls had no doors and a cast iron bath crouched at the centre. A cracked mirror leaned between floor and shadowy wall, reflecting her feet. A few sinks clung obstinately to filthy tiles. Sam tested for water, but found none.

Wind whistled around the upstairs rooms. A door or window slammed above them, making Rachel jump. Sam laughed and affectionately patted her shoulder. She grinned, self-mockingly. His pupils were huge and his smile gentle. Breaking the spell, she hurried past him, out of the room and back to her computer.

The office closed around her, shutting out the noises of the wind. Rachel zipped open her rucksack and removed a torch from it, playing with its weight in her hand.

She opened the internet browser and accessed Twitter. Bite-sized chunks of chatter opened out on the screen. She touched the keys lightly, not wishing to disturb the silence. Sam's footsteps clicked behind her.

Staying at abandoned asylum. Still daylight. Quiet so far. No sign of ghosts…yet.

Sunlight no longer penetrated the high window, and the flickering glow of Rachel's laptop became their only source of light. Feeling cold, Rachel pulled a sweater and a bar of chocolate from her rucksack. She offered half to Sam. He placed it in his mouth, smiling contentedly as the sweetness melted over his tongue.

'Come here,' he said, opening his arms.

Cheek resting against his chest, wrapped in his arms, Rachel felt that she too might melt. When he dropped his arms and took a step back, the warmth drained from her skin. She coughed and sat down in front of the laptop, checking for replies to her tweet.

- You're so brave #hauntedhouse

- Pics or it didn't happen.

'I'm going to wander around.'

'Do you want company?' Sam asked.

Perhaps too brusquely, she told him to keep track of replies.

She grabbed her torch and turned left, walking along the dimly lit corridor. She tiptoed, through an open doorway, into a large room. The windows in front of her faced west, and the room was filled with amber light, divided into tiger stripes by the steel bars bolted to the glass. To her left, was a wall and a dark archway. A glazed observation closet jutted out from the wall to her right. Rachel snapped a photo with her mobile phone and uploaded it to Twitter with the hashtag *abandoned_asylum*.

No furniture remained. The hushed tension of the space conjured imagined occupants, sitting about or pacing the room, unaware of each other. She heard a noise coming from the darkness beyond the archway. *An animal?* Curiosity pushed her to check, hoping to add spice to her next tweet. Fear held her back. Anything could have been lurking in the shadows. Embarrassed by the temptation to call Sam, she took one step closer and heard rustling. She paused, straining her hearing, trying to visualise the size, weight and position of the thing. It sounded small. At least its movements seemed small. Rachel edged closer, hovering between action and inaction. As the evening sun vanished behind trees she reached the centre of the room. The distance between her and the archway seemed to expand and contract. The sound shifted: a scratching sound, closer than before, to her right, beside or beyond the windows. She strode towards the opening.

Rachel flashed a torch-beam around the room. White light swept across a wheelchair, an overturned laundry trolley and, in the corner, a blackened teddy bear. She picked up the toy. Its fur damp and sticky. Recoiling, she released it and it thudded heavily on the floor. She rubbed her hand against the rough denim of her jeans, but could not shift the dark blue-green stain at the centre of her palm. Scratching her discoloured skin, she hurried back to her office sanctuary and Sam.

He stood up when he saw her. Instead of telling him what happened, she rushed to the laptop, eager to share the moment with the world. Typing furiously, careless of the noise, she wrote: *Scared by a bear. May need a tetanus. Heard noises. Getting dark now.*

'A bear?' Sam asked, reading over her shoulder.

'A teddy bear,' she replied. 'But a very scary teddy.'

He laughed and touched her hair. 'Show me.'

It took all her willpower to resist kissing his fingers. Instead she led him to the room and took the opportunity to upload an image of the offending teddy.

'Terrifying,' he agreed.

When they returned to the office Rachel broke another bar of chocolate into two generous pieces, thinking ruefully about the absence of alcohol in her rucksack.

'I wish I brought some beer.'

Sam retrieved two cans from his bag. He opened Rachel's before passing it to her.

She took a mouthful of slightly warm liquid and sat down. 'Thank you.'

Swallowing chocolate and gulping beer, she wondered where they should sleep. The thought of sitting shoulder to shoulder with Sam and dozing with their backs against the filing cabinet was tempting.

Rachel's pelvis grew heavy. She needed the toilet. The sudden realisation pushed her out of the office. Wind howled through the corridor. An open window slammed. She sprinted to the bathroom.

Finding the cleanest stall, she squatted over the porcelain bowl, careful not to touch it. Torchlight bounced around the room as she adjusted her position. When it hit the looking glass its beam illuminated the entire room. She placed the torch on the floor, pointing towards the mirror. The silvered glass was pitted with black acne and spider-web scratches. The reflected room appeared misty and unreal, the bathtub disjointed, like an incomplete jigsaw.

Finished, she stood and pulled up her jeans. A movement in the mirror caught her eye. The reflected bathtub appeared clearer. Snakes of steam rose from its curved rim. Within the mist, a dark dome of hair stood proud above the edge of the tub. Rachel stared at the real bath in panic. It was empty.

Wind groaned around the edges of the room, like the climactic scene in a zombie movie where the heroine becomes overcome by a crush of the undead. She pointed the light at the door and ran towards it.

Plop - the sound of a single drop of water falling. Her heart raced. *Where's Sam?* Instead of his hurried footsteps all she heard was the sucking sound of water releasing a body from its embrace. A wet foot hit the floor with a slap, then another. Slowly, the sounds moved towards her. She sensed the outstretched hands of a naked woman and dead, milky eyes staring ahead. The hairs on the back of her neck vibrated as thin, pale arms and fingers reached for her.

Screaming, she ran towards the office, slamming the door behind her and cracking its frosted-glass panel.

'What's wrong?' Sam asked. His eyelids strained against gravity. He pushed his slouched, sleep-filled body off the floor.

Shaking her head, Rachel sat in the swivel chair. Her palms clamped over her ears, she rocked herself slowly at first, then more and more ferociously. She dared not glance towards the door or even face Sam, acutely aware that the latter would place the door in her periphery vision.

'I saw something,' Rachel whispered.

'What did you see?' Sam asked.

She shrugged.

'I'll go and check,' Sam said.

The door groaned open. The handle clicked as he closed it behind him. Sam's footsteps moved away from her. She faced the door, to call him back, confess her terror. Through the cracked panel she saw the squashed features of a face pressed against the glass.

Help me, she typed. Rachel pressed the send button and prayed. The door-handle clicked sharply as something pushed it downwards. Cold, damp air rushed towards her.

'Help,' Rachel whispered as narrowed eyes peered at her. A green surgical mask filled with air then compressed against the curved lips of a cruel mouth. The figure stepped away from the door and towards Rachel. She shook her head to deny its presence. A hand lifted to touch her cheek. Cold fingers. She closed her eyes. Squeezed them shut. Waited.

'Rachel!'

Her eyes opened. Sam's expression morphed from a friendly smile to a mask of terror. His mouth hung open, stretching his face. She wanted to speak, to ask him what was wrong, but only exhaled putrid gas.

He backed away. The door creaked as he pushed against it with his shoulder. Then he was running along the corridor.

Rachel glanced back at the laptop before following. Its screen flickered urgently, willing her to action. Paper pressed against her lips. She pulled the mask from her mouth and flung it to the floor. Sam's footsteps echoed around the empty hallway. His shadow slipping into darkness as he fled. She sprinted after the bouncing beam of his torch. The light beckoned her. Her only salvation in this madhouse. She mustn't let him get away. She couldn't face being left alone here, not again.

Eat the Rich

Sally's call sounded desperate and confused. I peddled as quickly as I could to the crumbling multi-storey car park. It was deserted, as usual. Not a tourist hot spot. If cars didn't get damaged by falling chunks of concrete they would be stripped of their tyres within an hour of parking. I was surprised it hadn't been gentrified like the rest of the city, but no doubt that was someone's plan for the future.

They were on the basement level. Hazmat's gallery. More talented than Banksy but as yet undiscovered. As always I felt awe when I saw his work. A new piece had been started. A Doctor Marten boot kicking something that looked like a pig's head in a riot helmet. The blood spray looked particularly realistic.

Sally and Hazmat, my best friends and comrades. They accepted my weirdness and I loved them for it. Sally had a sort of post-punk Goth look with half her head shaven, and the other half a jungle of back-combed black hair set off by her Cleopatra-style kohl-smudged eyes. Hazmat was more your original 70s punk – green mohawk and black leather jacket. And me? I guess I was hard to explain.

Sally knelt beside Hazmat, pressing a cotton dressing

against his cheek. She glanced up at me and tried to focus her eyes.

"It's me," I assured her.

"He's in a bad shape, Grinch," Sally answered. Her pierced lips curling into a worried smile.

"What happened?"

Hazmat tilted a bottle of cider against his lips. "They're in worse shape," he claimed proudly, nodding towards his crumpled sleeping bag.

I spotted three skinheads beneath the filthy, once-red, nylon bedding. Their necks and arms covered in vile fascist tattoos, deep blood-encrusted caverns in their racist skulls. "Fucking Nazis."

"They attacked him while he was painting," Sally said. "He did that with his sodding paint can."

"Did they cut his face?" I asked.

"Bit it," Hazmat said. "Fucking animals."

Animals? Nah. Humans were much worse. Especially the fasch.

"He should go to hospital, but he won't. I've given him some meds and I'll get some more. He can't stay here though. He needs somewhere cleaner."

"My couch is a bit cleaner, I guess," I said.

"It's cleaner than mine," she agreed. "Let's take him there. What about them?"

"We'll tidy up then set fire to the bodies. No one gives

a fuck about a few dead Nazis. It's a bloody public service disposing of them," I said, meaning every word. "Love your new mural, Haz. The blood looks very real."

"It's theirs." His head bobbed forward. Cider and whatever drugs Sally had administered must have been working their magic on him. Immobile spikes of jade green crowned his exhausted head. *My fucking hero.*

I thought he was going to die. It seemed wrong not to take him to hospital even though he forbade it. Sally made sure he had the right antibiotics and pain relief, probably stronger than he would have got at Newham General. Who'd have known drug dealers made such great doctors? He was hallucinating and sweating profusely for thirty-six hours before his fever broke. When it did he looked older, thinner and impossibly pale.

"Nah, he's alright," Sally said. "I know people who would die for a pallor like that."

I snorted. "How are you feeling, Haz?"

"Like a fucking zombie," he said.

"You just need to eat something," Sally told him. "I'll grab some chips."

"Reckon I need some meat," he said.

I felt like I might vomit. "No meat," I told him. "Not in my house, you ass-hole." *Love would only permit so much. Eating animals under my roof? Not fucking likely.*

Sally seemed more sympathetic. "Maybe it's an iron deficiency. I'll see what I can get."

"Okay, but no meat. I mean it."

"I know you do, Grinchy poo. I solemnly promise never to bring the carcasses of slaughtered animals into your home."

Grinchy poo? I let it go. She was one of a tiny number of people I didn't want to punch. Since I'd been taking the T that had become a rare thing indeed. A fact that should probably have worried me more than it did.

She brought him dark green salad leaves and beetroot but he spat out the first and only mouthful.

He shook his head. "Fuck. I can't do it. Some thing's wrong with me. It's more than hunger. I dreamed terrible things. I dreamed of cracking skulls and shovelling down their contents. Sal, this bloody bandage itches. Can I take it off?"

"Let me look," Sally said. She peeled back the cotton gently then gasped.

"What is it?" Hazmat and I said in unison.

She didn't speak so I took a look.

"Bollocks!"

"What?" Hazmat asked. "What is it? Is it bad? Is it infected?"

"It's healed," I whispered. "Surely that can't be possible."

Sally shook her head.

He shrugged. "I feel really restless. I need to get out of here. I want a fight and I'd rather it weren't with you, Grinch."

"I'm sure I could take you anyway."

He laughed.

"A bunch of us are sabotaging a hunt this afternoon. I was gonna bail, with you so sick and all, but if you're feeling better ... Plenty of rich wankers to punch while we wait for the next Nazi to come along. Direct your anger where it counts."

Hazmat grinned. His eyes shone in a way that would give me nightmares.

They were there with rifles, dogs and horses, the arrogant bastards. We shouted, threatened and generally got in the way. It was an impasse and it frustrated the hell out of the hunters. They were used to getting their way, and looked like they'd be happy to shoot us all – punks, anarchists and hippies alike.

Hazmat was bristling. It wasn't only the hair of his mohawk that stood on end. I could tell he wanted action. I felt just as excited. This was class war and animal rights activism rolled into one delicious bundle.

One of them felt brave enough to approach. We faced off, him with his rifle, us with our righteous anger. I felt

Hazmat lurch beside me. I touched his arm, and he rewarded me with a deep scratch that drew blood. He pounced. I never imagined a human being could jump like that. The riding hat flew into the trees, and Haz dragged the rich bloke to the ground. His skull cracked open like an egg shell. I couldn't see much of the attack as Hazmat's muscled torso blocked my view. It was only when he got up again, blood dripping from his mouth and covering his "Eat the Rich" t-shirt, that I saw the devastation. I vomited. Doubled over I heard screams all around me. People fled. Dogs growled. Horses panicked and kicked out, dislodging their riders. The sound of bones crunching replaced the screams of terror and I fell unconscious.

I was back in my bedsit when I came to. Hazmat had showered and dressed in clean clothes. For a blissful moment I laughed at the vividness of my dream. Of course it hadn't been real. *Hazmat didn't just eat someone. Ridiculous.* This wasn't Hollywood, it was East London. My arm itched. I tried to scratch it but there was a bandage in the way.

"What's this?" I asked.

"Sorry, mate," Hazmat said, looking ashamed. "I think I scratched you. Sally patched you up, but it's a bit yellow and smells rotten. She asked me to give you some antibiotics when you woke up. I didn't tell her about what I did at the hunt. Do you think I should? Those toffs tasted so good, mate."

"You ate them? Bollocks. I thought … Shit!"

"And you wanted me meat free. They were probably free range though, Grinch. And I only ate part of them."

"Which part?"

"Their brains … I'm a zombie aren't I? Diseased Nazi scum bites me and now I'm the living dead. Well fuck it. I always said I wanted to eat the rich."

He handed me the pills.

"Does this mean I'll be like you?"

He shrugged. "I don't fuckin' know how it works, mate. Sorry though. It looks pretty deep. Are you in pain?"

I shook my head. "It just itches." I swallowed the pill.

"Like my face."

Thirty-six hours later, I was hungry for brains.

It sucked, but there were ways I could turn this to my advantage. I sprayed up my white quiff and pulled on my favourite striped jeans. I filled the pockets with as many coins as I could find around the bedsit. Admittedly it was no fortune, but all I needed was an in. Then I headed out, into the city.

You don't have to look for long in London to find those of our brethren without roofs over their heads. The great ignored. I'd often considered them a potentially unstoppable army come the revolution. My idea, if it worked, would just bring the revolution a lot closer.

The first poor bastard stank of piss. The ammonia hurt my nose, but out of respect I refused to show any signs of repulsion. I sat next to him on the shallow front step of a Georgian town house with twelve door bells. He looked at my coolly.

"Are you a boy or a girl?" he asked.

Always the same question. "Neither," I answered. "But I could be your power animal. I can make you so strong you can take everything you need from those rich wankers who pass you by with their noses in the air."

"Are you some sort of pervert?"

I laughed. *Only as much as the next person,* I guessed. "Let me get you a coffee and you can listen while you warm your belly."

"You've got a deal. Don't skimp on the sugar though."

It didn't take as long as I expected to convince him. I suppose he had nothing left to lose and the thought of paying back in kind all the cops who had kicked or pushed him around sold him on my idea. I scratched his hand and left him with antibiotics. I would have preferred to gather my army in a large shelter, but that wasn't within my means. So I gave him the address of Hazmat's basement gallery and asked him to meet me there the following evening. As I walked away towards my next recruit, I hoped he'd survive the night.

It pained me to know what people would let me do in exchange for a hot beverage. Lack of shelter and regular food dehumanised people, and many of those I spoke to seemed to have lost all sense of self. Each day was just about survival to them, avoiding violence and eating the scraps they were given. This in a city where one bedroom apartments sold for millions. It was obscene. I bought dozens of coffees and administered almost as many scratches. I could only bring myself to do it with their consent. It would be like pyramid selling, I reckoned. *First I scratch ten per day, then each recruit converts ten per day, and within a week we'll have over 20,000 super-strong zombie soldiers.*

After they turned, the zombies hung out together in the abandoned car park, getting increasingly hungry and frustrated. There were the inevitable casualties, but if I might be allowed to say it myself - it was fucking awesome. I made Hazmat very proud. An outcast army eager to wreak havoc and destruction. A nihilist's wet dream. In my mind we were simply soldiers in the class war and we would all be tested in battle the following evening.

Thousands of bodies swarmed together along city streets towards the palace, like one homogeneous mass with a hive mind. It was more than a mob. It was life. Police in riot gear mobilised quickly and blocked the road ahead, twenty or more rows deep. They weren't taking our march lightly. I'm sure they intended to provoke the peasants into violence and arrest our asses. *Be careful what you wish for.* I felt no fear. I felt indestructible. Hazmat and Sally on either side. No longer strictly vegan, but with a very specialised diet.

We were demanding our human right to food, shelter and dignity. It was immaterial that our dietary requirements were human brains. Beyond the armoured pigs, great gates stood before Buckingham Palace, an ostentatious symbol of our oppression when we were still human. Once their riot helmets had been removed the police would be zombie food, followed by the Queen's guard. We would eat well this evening. We would climb the gates, supported by our comrades and swarm onto the property. *God save the fucking Queen, from us!*

The juddering of rubber bullets and live ammunition asked a question – how dare you come here? I could smell victory in the cranial fluids that washed down each mouthful of grey matter. I was dining on pork for the first time in over a decade. Blood lust rose inside me and I tore helmets, often with heads still attached, from the Metropolitan Police's shoulders. We bathed in a shower of gore, the zombie punks, the militarised homeless and the rest of the hooligans. *La Terreur* in Paris over 200 years before could not have tasted more sweet. The guillotine could not have been a more efficient executioner than our arms and teeth.

Hazmat grinned at me as he separated another cop from its helmet.

I grinned back then shrugged. "Hey guys. Tomorrow we're homeless. Tonight it's a blast!"

"Or we're living in a fucking palace," Sally whispered in my ear.

I was shoved with a riot shield and knocked into my friend. She fell backward, landing on her ass. I tried to reach for her. But she shook her head and laughed. "All good here," she shouted. "Carry on." She sprang to her feet and slammed forward like she was in a mosh pit. Fucking punks. I loved them all to bits. You couldn't keep them down. Alive or undead.

Armoured vans, water cannons and SWAT teams descended on Green Park and St James Park as we munched through the riot police and clambered over the gates. Busbies, red jackets and bayonets charged at us. Some blades reaching their mark and felling us. Others aiming ineffectively at our chests. Behind us bullets whizzed through the air, hitting our backs and limbs. Water tried to knock us off our feet but made the Queen's soldiers fall on their asses instead. We descended on them like starving wolves, sating more than hunger as blood lust rose in each zombie.

My phone beeped. So did a hundred others. I fished into my jeans and pulled it out. Smeared blood across the screen. Emergency message. For their own safety, everyone must return to and stay in their homes until further notice. Was it just London on shut down or all over the country? I screamed with excitement. A stupid grin plastered across my face, I glanced around.

Those human comrades who were still alive looked afraid. This was no normal riot. I watched them flee, invariably ending up caught and loaded into police vans. I wondered whether anyone would believe the stories they'd tell. I wondered how many of us would survive this night. I wondered why I didn't care.

I had enough to care about. The hiss of skin tearing from muscle. The smell of blood and intestines. Hot viscera hitting my face. I closed powerful jaws around parietal bones and heard them crack as I exerted pressure. Blood hit my throat first then the spongy mush of cranial matter. A thousand electrical pulses shot around my head like a lightning ball and energy surged through neurons to every nerve ending making me shiver deliciously. I hooked finger nails under broken bits of skull to remove bone fragments and plunged my face into the makeshift bowls to dine. Over and over again. Each experience seemed new and unique, each taste sublime. I lost myself. My intellect fled and I forgot where I was. The doors gave way under our combined pressure and I darted through red and gold rooms. Between portraits and mirrors. Under arches full of skylights. I followed the scent of blood and human sweat, the sound of beating hearts. The gaudy gold and ugly paintings couldn't hold my attention. I only wanted to feed again.

I heard the rotary blades of a helicopter. Blindly I ran, tearing my way through drapes and panelled doors, relying on my senses of smell and hearing. Others moved with me. Although I couldn't recognise their faces in my rage, I knew they were of my kind and would not provide me with my next meal. The helicopter noise retreated. It was airborne. Presumably taking humans to safety. But some remained. I could smell them. Hear them whimper.

Smoke rushed into the room. It tasted like vinegar and made me screw up my face. I retreated from the open doors, past rows of chairs and toward a dais and the thrones. Boots hit the floor hard, echoing between walls. Plastic shields taller than me, pushed through the ornate archway and gathered to form a wall. Behind them insect-like gas masks and helmet mounted torches glared at me. I fled to a door on my right and out of the room, chased by the sound of dozens of rubber soles hitting marble. This room was filled with the slow rolling mist as well. I'd encountered it before. Last time it made my eyes burn, my nose run and my chest threaten to implode. This time it was just a nasty smell that overwhelmed all other scents. With my ears full of footsteps and my nose full of tear gas I had no idea where the whimpering humans were hiding. Other zombies ran blindly through the corridor, equally disorientated. I recognised Hazmat as he stumbled over to me. His right foot bent at a strange angle. I pulled his arm over my shoulders and hurried him along.

The palace was a warren of hundreds perhaps thousands of rooms. The mist had permeated all of them. It was time to get out. A security camera followed our movements as we lurched into a room I hoped would lead to an outer wall, but again the only windows were far above us. I was sick of this place, of the smell, of the sounds, and the gold shining everywhere. But we were so lost. More doors, more rooms, yellow this time and at last tapestry drapes on the far wall. Together Hazmat and I hit the window with an ornate chair that shattered into pieces as it hit the glass. I grabbed a candelabra and used it as a battering ram. The pane splintered and we took it in turns to kick at the weak spot until at last the window smashed and we climbed out.

There were soldiers here too. They pounded us with bullets as we ran to the wall. It was high, but I'd seen Hazmat leap and was sure he could make it. We threw ourselves at the unforgiving stone and clawed our way to the railings at the top. I looked back and saw piles of dead.

Retreat and regroup, that was the plan. I hoped Sally would make it out.

Smoke filled the skyline and sirens wailed in every direction. The idea of fleeing for safety seemed ridiculous now. Instead we headed towards Downing Street. London was burning and we were hungry. It would be one hell of a barbecue.

226

Cellar Door

When the air creaked, my mouth gaped between my bulging eyes and hammering chest. 'Did you hear that?' I asked, nostrils flaring.

'Yes,' Carl replied. 'Was that what you heard before?'

'No. It was more of a rattle. I'm glad you heard it too this time. I was starting to worry that I was losing my mind.'

'Sorry I didn't believe you ... before.'

'You believed me enough to come down here with me.'

He was silent for a moment. His eyes flicked from left to right as if weighing options. 'Full disclosure. I had ulterior motives for following you down here.'

'Oh?' I focused on the wooden stairs that led back to the kitchen, wondering whether I would reach them in time. 'What motives?'

'Nothing bad.'

Twenty-four hours earlier, Carl, Yolanda and I sat in front of a wood fire in the bijoux kitchen. Four doors led out of the room, five if you included the quaint pantry we'd filled with food a couple of hours before. I knew Yolanda from college and she'd invited me on this trip, with her brother, when she'd discovered my lack of plans for the holiday. Already I suspected her of trying to set us up. Carl was handsome enough, but I couldn't see beyond his thick beard and dreadlocked hair, a comfortable match for the rustic charm of our cabin, I guessed.

The bitter sweet coffee wasn't keeping my tiredness at bay. Yolanda's and my bedroom was upstairs, one of the doors led to a narrow staircase. Carl would be sleeping in a downstairs room, complete with bed-settee, which might have served as a living room for smaller parties.

A third door led outside to a sheltered porch where we'd sat and chatted until cold mist descended half an hour before. The final door was bolted on this side. I'd peeked behind it to see a set of even narrower stairs, leading to what I assumed was the cellar. The air that greeted me smelled of fungus and made me shiver. Carl had asked me to lock it and we hadn't opened it a second time.

I caught a yawn in my hand. 'I'm sorry. It's been a long day.'

'Travelling always takes it out of you.' Yolanda raked long fingers through her curls. 'We'll turn in soon.'

'I might use the bathroom first, if that's okay,' I suggested.

'Be our guest,' Carl said. 'See you in the morning.'

I collapsed on a single bed, let my eyes adjust to the gloom and listened to Yolanda move about in the very basic bathroom, brushing her teeth and spitting. I let my eyes close and my body sink into the soft mattress, feeling very optimistic about the holiday.

A sharp noise followed by, 'Ouch! Shit! Sorry,' pulled me back to consciousness.

'Are you okay?' I asked, sitting up.

'I just bashed my ankle.'

'Do you want to switch the light on?'

'It's okay. I found my bed,' Yolanda whispered.

'Goodnight.'

'Goodnight, Kate.'

I lay in bed with my eyes wide open. A faint light shone beyond the patterned curtains. It seemed to move subtly, highlighting different shapes, I assumed it was the wind moving tree branches, which partially blocked the moonlight, or my tired mind playing tricks, but I couldn't relax. I watched the window and sensed it was observing me in return. The patterns in the curtains resembled faces in this light. Demonic faces, trying to come in from the cold. The window rattled against the wind. "Let us in," it said. I pulled the blankets over my face and reminded myself I was perfectly safe, with my friends, at the start of a relaxing break. Eventually I must have fallen asleep.

I woke to the smell of coffee. Sunlight shone through the curtains highlighting a heavy paisley pattern, not faces at all.

Yolanda's bed was empty so I strode to the window and opened the curtains wide, allowing warm rays to flood into the timber room, bathing me in their light as they nudged past. The wind had dropped and tree branches as still as statues reached for the sky. Beyond the closest four trees a metallic blue Land Rover was parked on the dirt track. I opened the window and let in bird song. This place was idyllic. Too good to be true, my paranoia warned. We were in the middle of nowhere. *Yes, but with no stress or responsibilities other than to have fun. Perfect.* The matter settled, at least for now, I pulled on a pair of jeans and hurried downstairs to Yolanda and coffee.

'Did you sleep well?' she asked.

I nodded and poured coffee into my mug, followed by three heaped spoons of sugar. Well it was my first cup and the energy boost was welcome. 'Is Carl still asleep?'

'He went fishing first thing,' Yolanda said.

'Salmon for breakfast?' I asked, hopefully.

'If you're lucky we may have trout for dinner. There aren't any salmon is this river.'

'So what's the plan for today?'

'I thought we'd take a walk in the forest. Wildlife photography and exercise. Does that sound good to you?'

It did. 'Perfect. Can we swim in the river?'

'If it warms up enough later,' she said. 'The mist has cleared but it's still chilly.'

The coffee pot was empty so I decided to brew some more while I made toast for breakfast.

'Bottled water,' Yolanda reminded me.

I nodded. I'd been warned not to use the taps for drinking water. 'Thank you for bringing me here.'

'You needed to get away,' she said. 'And you can't get more away than this.'

I breathed in deeply, inhaling clean air. Yolanda moved quietly, camera always at the ready. She reminded me of a hunter and I watched her sinewy frame stretch and bend then hunch and squat as new movements in undergrowth or canopy caught her eye. I sat on the rough wool blanket we'd spread beneath an oak, watching her more than the wildlife, gently amused by her lack of self-consciousness.

Eventually she joined me on the blanket.

'Did you catch anything?' I asked.

'Some wonderful insects and a hare. I'll have to get them onto the laptop to see how good they are, but I think it's a great start.'

'Will you try and get them published?'

She nodded. 'How else am I supposed to pay for the trip?'

I felt guilty. I hadn't paid her anything to come on holiday. Had she expected me to?

Perhaps she read my thoughts or more likely I

communicated worry through my tight jaw and pinched mouth.

'It's okay.' She laughed. 'I didn't mean that. Just relax and enjoy yourself, okay.'

'Thank you.'

'Te nada.'

We stopped by the river on the way back. The brim of Carl's hat shaded his eyes from the sun. I couldn't tell, from this angle, whether he was intently watching the river or sleeping. Yolanda crept up behind him.

'Catch anything?'

The way he jumped at her voice made me think he'd been sleeping. 'Not yet.'

'Good job we're not relying on you for dinner then.'

He grinned. His teeth gleamed between a perfect curve of lips. My heart leaped and heat rose in my cheeks and elsewhere.

'Good morning, Kate,' he said.

'Good m-m-morning,' I stammered. 'Did you sleep well?'

'As well as to be expected.'

'Couch not comfy?'

'It's okay. How were the beds?'

'Like lying on a cloud,' Yolanda answered. 'But at least you've been catching up on your zees, right bro?'

He nodded. 'My belly tells me it's lunch time. I'll pack up.'

I thought I saw a dark shape dart around the end of the line, but Carl didn't get a bite. Maybe it was a shadow or something not interested in his bait. I shivered.

'Cold?' he asked.

Yolanda returned to my side and took my hand. 'We'll meet you back at the cabin.'

'I won't be long,' he answered.

We prepared a simple feast of bread and cheese. Neither of us waited for Carl to return before stuffing our faces. It was good, wholesome food and the walk had prepared us for a frenzied feeding.

'So hungry,' I spluttered through crumbs.

'It's the fresh air,' Yolanda replied. 'Eat as much as you want. It's not like we're going to get fat out here.'

'Carl's been a while.'

'Maybe he got a bite,' she said.

'I did see something in the river.'

'That's probably it then. Maybe we'll have fish for dinner after all,' Yolanda said.

Carl still hadn't returned by the time our bellies were full.

'Should I go and check?' I asked.

'Do you remember the way?'

I nodded.

'Okay then. I'll get these photos onto the laptop while you're gone. See what I got.'

When I reached the river bank it was empty. I knelt at the edge where Carl's ass had crushed the grass and watched the slow flowing water ooze past. He must have taken a different route back. I dipped the tips of my fingers into the stream and realised immediately why Yolanda had been less than confident about swimming. The icy chill was painful and my fingers glowed red when I quickly withdrew my hand. A dark shape darted below the surface. It was huge. If Carl caught it, that fish would feed us for days. I stood up and brushed soft earth from my knees. If I didn't head back soon they might assume I'd got lost. The path was easy to follow and in less than ten minutes I saw the cabin rise from behind the trees.

Yolanda grinned. 'I've got some good ones here. Come see.'

I walked around the heavy table. 'Where's Carl?'

She frowned. 'What do you mean? You were going to fetch him.'

'He wasn't there. I thought I'd missed him, taken a different route.'

She shook her head. 'Off daydreaming, no doubt. I'm sure he'll be back soon.'

'Shouldn't we go and check?'

'Give him thirty minutes before we start to worry. Look at this hare. Isn't he splendid?'

The picture was magnificent. I hadn't realised Yolanda was such a talented photographer.

'Very regal,' I said.

'Yes, regal, that's the word I was searching for. King of the forest.'

'I saw a monster fish in the river.'

Her eyes were sharp. 'Monster?'

'It was huge. It would feed twenty I reckon.'

'Nice,' she said relaxing. 'Do you know what kind of fish or was it an eel?'

'No clue. It was just big. Remember I'm a city girl.'

She smiled, indulgently. 'You might not feel that way after a week in the wild.'

The door opened and Carl slouched in.

'Kate was starting to worry,' Yolanda said.

'Aww, that's sweet. Did you miss me?'

I shrugged. 'I just wanted to make sure you got lunch.'

'Looks good,' he said. 'I'll just go and clean up.'

He came back with washed hands and clean clothes, but the scent of damp earth still hung around him. It wasn't an unpleasant smell, just unexpected.

'Where did you go?' I asked.

'Huh?'

'Kate came to fetch you for lunch. You weren't at the

river. I told her you were probably daydreaming somewhere,' Yolanda said.

'You know me too well, sis. Were you worried?'

'I wasn't,' Yolanda said, pointedly.

'No need to worry about me, Katie. I know these woods like the back of my hand. You could say we sorta grew up here, Yolanda and I.'

'Really?'

'No,' Yolanda said.

I looked at Carl, but he had his mouth and hands full. Last thing I wanted to do was disturb a hungry man while eating.

Carl and I played cards around the kitchen table while heavy rain battered the roof. Yolanda edited the photos she planned to send to magazines and backed them up on a USB card attached to her keyring. The quality of her photos shocked me. Ashamed that I hadn't known this about her before. Two years as my best friend and it seemed I'd hardly scratched the surface of her complexity. I'd spent too much time telling her about myself and not enough asking questions. I resolved to be a more interested friend from now on.

With no fish, we dined on chick peas and sweet potato served on a bed of rice. I was relieved, to tell the truth, I wasn't certain whether I would manage raking through the bones of a freshly caught fish, however delicious it might smell. Carl had cooked, brilliantly I should add. I tried not to let the siblings' talents make me feel inadequate, but it wasn't easy. Part of me wanted to prove myself worthy and I hoped I'd find ample opportunity to do so over the next five days.

Darkness fell. The world shrunk around our cabin as if the circle of trees marked the end of the Earth. We sat on the porch comfortable with our own silence and listening to the hoots of owls, the steady pitter patter of raindrops, and rustling of trees. I nestled against Yolanda's arm, breathing in the salty scent of her skin and the musk of her hair. Carl sat on a wooden chair on the other side of the porch, watching us intently.

I yawned, embarrassing myself.

'Have we worn you out?' Yolanda asked.

'It's just so relaxing here,' I said. 'I wish I could stay forever.'

Silence followed, but it wasn't awkward, Carl's wide smile assured me.

Another yawn pressed against my larynx. 'Maybe I should head for bed.'

'Goodnight, Kate, sleep well,' Carl said.

Yolanda simply kissed my forehead and with that I scrambled up the stairs.

Having seen the faces in our window the night before, I searched for them again as I sank into bed. They hung above the narrow ledge, poised as if ready to pounce. Reality and fantasy merged as I realised they looked an awful lot like my two friends.

I sat up, my ears straining, wondering if the heavy sound had been in my dreams or had come from downstairs. Yolanda purred in her sleep, the blanket tucked tight around her. A dream then, but try as I might I couldn't settle. I hunted in the dark for my clothes and tiptoed down the stairs.

The fluorescent bulb blinked before illuminating the kitchen. I pushed the door shut behind me and filled a glass with water from the fridge. Heavy footsteps then the creak of a door opening made my hairs stand on end. Wearing only a pair of cotton shorts, Carl hovered in the doorway.

'I'm sorry. I didn't mean to wake you. I thought I heard a noise.'

He rubbed his eyes. 'It's okay. Are you heading back to bed?'

'Not yet. Unless I'm disturbing you.'

'Not at all. Mind if I sit with you?' he asked.

I nodded. 'Thanks. That would be nice.'

'I'll grab some warmer clothes and be right back.'

I watched the muscular crease above the line of his boxers as he walked away then splashed cold water on my cheeks before refilling my glass. He returned as I was sitting down again, wrapped now in a jumper and sweatpants. Small framed glasses rested on the hooked bridge of his wide nose. They suited him, although I had no idea he needed glasses. They made him look wise and gentle like an old wizard.

'I usually wear contacts,' he said.

I had no idea what to say. I found his presence intimidating. I breathed easier as he sat at the other side of the table, hiding his powerful bulk.

I heard the noise again like a metal door being shaken. As a kid I used to enjoy skipping across the metal trapdoors that led to cellars below bars and public houses. They made sharp, grating sounds accompanied by hollow echoes. This noise was the same, but more persistent and it made the hairs on the back of my neck stand on end.

'Did you hear that?'

Carl shook his head.

'I think it came from downstairs. I'm going to investigate. Maybe there's an animal trapped down there.'

'I didn't hear anything,' Carl insisted.

'I won't be able to sleep if I don't check.'

'I'll come with you. I'm not sure how well it is lit. Maybe we should take a torch. Wait a minute.'

I pulled back the bolt and waited for Carl to return. The door vibrated as if a storm was brewing inside.

'Are you sure about this?' he asked.

'Are you scared?'

He shrugged. 'Bad memories.'

'What sort of memories?'

'I got locked down there when I was a kid.'

'Really?'

He shifted uncomfortably from foot to foot and stared at the floor.

'You don't have to come with me,' I offered.

'I'm okay,' he said at last.

'Maybe we should find something to stop the door shutting behind us?'

'It's okay. It can't lock itself accidentally.'

'Are you sure?' I asked, not wanting to get trapped.

'Yes, absolutely.'

I squeezed my lips together as I always did when I needed to be brave. 'Okay, are you ready?'

He nodded. 'I'm ready.'

I opened the door. Foul air wrapped itself around me. Presumably the rain had got down here, because it smelled damper than before and colder than a tomb. I shouted, hoping to attract the attention of whatever was there without having to brave the stairs. 'Helloooo!'

I thought I heard a faint shuffling, but when I looked to Carl to check whether he had heard it too he just shrugged.

'I think there's a light switch on the right there,

somewhere,' he said.

It was an old fashioned switch, one of those smooth, cool, Bakelite deals, with a hard nipple and a lever action that clicked into place before a pale flickering glow allowed me to see thirteen wooden treads, none of which appeared rotten. 'Okay then,' I said more to myself than Carl and I took the first step.

While the stairs were dry the ground at the bottom squelched and I sank a fraction before hitting rough concrete. 'Euch.' Why hadn't I put shoes on?

Carl's breath ruffled my hair and I moved forward to let him descend. 'It must have flooded,' he said. He switched on the torch and swept the ceiling with its beam. 'Can't see where the water got in though.'

'May I?' I asked and took the torch from his shaking hand. 'You can go back up if you want.'

His hand skimmed across my shoulder before it fell to his side. 'And let you face an angry badger on your own? I don't think so.'

'You think it's a badger?'

'I don't know, but I guess it could be. Maybe it dug its way in here somehow and can't find a way back out.'

'It sounded big.'

'Badgers are pretty big bastards.'

'Is it safe?' I asked.

'Dunno. Give me the torch back and I'll go first.'

I clung to the light. 'No. It's okay. Let's just listen for a moment.'

When the air creaked, my mouth gaped between my bulging eyes and hammering chest. 'Did you hear that?' I asked, nostrils flaring.

'Yes,' Carl replied. 'Was that what you heard before?'

'No. It was more of a rattle. I'm glad you heard it too this time. I was starting to worry that I was losing my mind.'

'Sorry I didn't believe you ... before.'

'You believed me enough to come down here with me.'

He was silent for a moment. His eyes flicked from left to right as if weighing options. 'Full disclosure. I had ulterior motives for following you down here.'

'Oh?' I focused on the wooden stairs that led back to the kitchen, wondering whether I would reach them in time. 'What motives?'

'Nothing bad. Just thought I'd do the hero thing.'

I laughed awkwardly. 'Wanted to get me all to yourself?'

He snorted. 'Hmm, if you want to put it that way.'

Tension squeezed my rib cage. I had no idea how to reply. 'Let's find that badger,' I said, eventually.

It wasn't a large space, but there were rows of shelving to check behind. As I moved around I felt colder and colder. My toes were numb and my shoulders shook, making the torchlight dart about spasmodically. Carl stepped closer and the upper half of my body warmed a little.

'Want my jumper?' Carl asked.

'I'm fine,' I answered.

Scrape …

'It came from there.' I pointed at some shelves loaded with half disintegrated cardboard boxes, blocking the wall behind. I told myself to move towards it, but found I was rooted to the spot.

'Allow me,' Carl said, prising the torch from my fingers.

The stair light didn't reach me and the torch was moving further away. I was swallowed by a darkness that didn't make sense based on the size of the cellar. The torch beam flickered then went out.

'Damn!' Carl's voice sounded distant.

Something wet and heavy slid swiftly across my bare foot. I screamed. Heading for the light and the stairs, I slipped and slid but managed to stay vertical. I reached the bottom tread and stood there trying to penetrate the darkness with my eyes.

'Carl?'

No reply.

'Carl? Carl, answer me please. This isn't funny.'

Silence.

'Say something or I'm going?'

Still nothing. The silence was a great weight I carried on my shoulders. I knew I should go and help him. He might have fallen, bashed his head, but the thought of the slippery monster kept my feet from straying from the relative safety of the wooden stair. I convinced myself that Carl was playing a prank. Any minute he'd come towards me, laughing at my fear. I waited for the punchline for what seemed like an hour but may have only been a minute.

'Carl?' There was no strength to my voice any longer. I doubt anyone would have heard me.

The clang of metal hitting metal sent me scuttling up the stairs like a cockroach. In the kitchen my fingers hovered over the bolt, but I couldn't lock him in there, could I? He'd come with me to help or possibly seduce me, either way he'd faced his fear of the cellar and I shouldn't betray that.

I had two options, hunt for another torch and head back down, this time wearing shoes and my coat, or wake Yolanda and ask for her help. I delayed choosing and sat on a wooden chair by the cold fireplace, staring at the unlocked door. The door didn't move. The metal sounds didn't return, but neither did Carl.

I am too ashamed to admit how long I sat there like that. All that time Carl could have been bleeding to death and I did nothing to save him. I wanted to get Yolanda, but in some deep recess of my psyche I knew the door would open as soon as I stopped watching it and the monsters would get me. I wanted to call her downstairs, but doing so would mean confessing my cowardice, and possibly my responsibility for her brother's death. She would surely hate me. She'd never understand. What I did, seemed at the time to be the lesser of all evils, or so I told myself. I crossed the kitchen and bolted the door then headed upstairs to wake my friend.

'Yolanda,' I called and switched on the bedroom light.

The faces receded from the curtains and the light threw shadows over the creases of Yolanda's blanket. She didn't stir. I took the opportunity to dress warmly before I patted the crease I assumed covered her shoulder. My fingers pushed the bedding down to the mattress beneath. I pulled back the covers to expose her empty bed. An indent from head to foot suggested some weight had lain there in the night, but no one and nothing slept there now.

'Shit!'

I looked out of the window, just in case Yolanda was outside, but it was too dark to see anything and dawn was still hours away. I couldn't catch my breath. My head too light and my body too heavy. What the fuck was I supposed to do now? I sat on the edge of my bed and tried to calm down. Carl was locked in the cellar. We'd gone in there because I'd heard a noise. I'd assumed Yolanda was asleep, no I didn't assume, I'd heard her snore, or something. I'd heard something. But Yolanda wasn't here now. Where was she?

I closed my eyes and concentrated on taking deeper, slower breaths. I heard laughter, but it might have been my imagination. Was Yolanda in on it too? Were they both playing a trick on me? No. That was too cruel and Yolanda was my friend, my only friend. I was the butt of everyone else's jokes and Yolanda had taken me under her wing, shown me I was someone worth knowing. Unless that was a lie, a plot, to get me here and play this trick on me. It was elaborate, unlikely, but it was possible, and what other solution was there to the absence of both my friends? If Yolanda had been in the cellar she might have made those noises. Then it was only a matter of getting me down there. Getting something, a dead fish maybe, to touch my foot and they would see the real me, the coward, the frightened child. Oh what fun! What a scream! They were probably filming it too. I'd be the star of YouTube. Running away, sobbing, shaking. Why else would she have asked me here?

I shook my head, but the thoughts wouldn't be deterred. They hadn't planned on my locking them in there though. Their trick had backfired. If I let them out would they laugh at me or apologise? If I let them out ...

A grin spread across my face and I wrapped the blankets around my body, cosy now, warmed by the knowledge that they weren't going to make a fool out of me.

They had messed with the wrong girl. Well they could stay down there tonight and I'd decide in the morning whether to let them out.

While my night was disturbed by the occasional knocking and clamouring, my self-satisfaction comforted me and I slept remarkably well.

I took my time packing my luggage and luxuriating in a hot bath, before I descended to the kitchen. I searched Carl's room and found the keys to the Land Rover on a Welsh Dresser. I filled the car with the things I needed and tucked the keys into my pocket before filling the kettle for coffee. As I sat at the small table, cradling the warm cup, I thought about what to do next.

There was no sound from beyond the cellar door and it was firmly bolted on this side. There was no sign of Yolanda and I became more convinced that brother and sister were waiting on the other side of the door for me. I made some toast, partly because I was hungry and partly because the smell might drive them to speak to me, beg me to let them out. I sated my hunger, but not my curiosity.

If I drove away I could return to college, finish my studies and pretend that none of this had happened. That's what the voices in my head advised. But things were never that simple, were they? Surely at some point Carl and Yolanda would escape the cellar and come after me. Unless they were dead. Even if they were, eventually someone would find their bodies. Someone would know I had come to the cabin with them and left alone. If Carl and Yolanda didn't find me then someone else would.

I could open the door and let them out. Pretend that I had been so scared I hadn't known what to do. That was at least partly true. If they were hurt then they would have learned a valuable lesson. If they laughed then at least the worst of it would be over. The joke had backfired anyway. They should be more humiliated than me by this point.

Or I might open the door and find nobody there. What would I do then? How could I sleep at night? How could I leave? How could I stay?

I realised after my third coffee that there was no perfect ending to this story. Whatever I did now would haunt me. My anger last night had blinded me, but now the weight of responsibility crushed both my schadenfreude and anxiety into a solid mass the size of a golf ball that clogged my arteries and blocked my windpipe. I walked across to the door. With my shaking fingertips against the bolt I called out.

'Carl, Yolanda, is anyone there?'

I pressed my ear against the wood. I heard hissing, but it may have been an echo of my blood.

What now?

I retrieved my mobile phone from the car, even though

I knew there would be no signal. I wasn't wrong. If it had worked I could have phoned Yolanda, the police, or my mum, but it didn't. More alone than ever, I pulled the keys from my pocket and toyed with the idea of leaving. There must be a signal a few miles away. I could stop there and decide what to do. I closed my eyes and saw Yolanda bleeding out on the cellar floor, her dead brother curled up beside her. No! That wasn't right. I was the victim here, not them. If they were hurt it was their fault. I climbed into the car and put the keys in the ignition. I just sat there, on the driver's seat, watching the key chain swing beside the steering column. Listening to it tap, tap, tap as it bounced against the dashboard. Tap, tap, tap, "let us in".

Sighing, I climbed out of the jeep and headed back to the cabin. I grabbed a knife from the drawer, just in case. In case of what? I had no idea. I reached up to pull back the bolt, and discovered it wasn't locked. Had I pulled it back earlier? I didn't think so. But I must have. It was painful to swallow. A golf ball heavy in my chest. I reached for the door knob and heard a car engine roar into life.

Relief lifted my cheeks and the golf ball cleared. Someone was coming. Someone to save me. Help me clear up this mess. I ran out onto the porch, just in time to watch the blue Land Rover drive away.

'Shit!'

'Shit! Shit! Shit!'

I ran after it. My heart pounding. 'Wait!'

My thighs were on fire and my ankles juddered each time my foot hit the soft ground to propel me forward, but the car was further and further ahead until it was lost among trees.

I hobbled back to the cabin, having no other place to go. I wanted to open the cellar door but I was too afraid. The room was spinning. I held onto walls for support and made my way to the bed-settee in Carl's room. The air still smelled of him. I rested my head on the calico arm rest and closed my eyes.

It was dark when I woke. My body shuddered with cold. My mouth bone dry. I had no strength to stand. My body wobbled so fiercely that I decided to crawl to the kitchen to get myself a drink. Sweat dripped off my nose. The floor was closer than I thought and scraped the skin from my hands and knees each time I misjudged the distance and slammed my limbs against the floorboards. Somehow I reached Carl's door and knelt up to open it. I had to shuffle to get through the narrow crack I'd managed to open. The kitchen was full of dense fog. It pressed against my mouth and nostrils, exerted pressure against my eyeballs and eardrums. My brain writhed like a bed of snakes and the fierce noise of hissing was everywhere. I shook until my limbs no longer supported me and landed heavily on my belly, forcing the air from my lungs with an even louder hiss. Between the table legs I saw the cellar door, wide open and darkness beyond.

Thirst like broken glass in my throat, it took all my strength to pull myself up to the sink. Thankfully there were clean mugs on the draining board and I filled the same one three times from the tap. The water was cloudy, but it dulled the pain and only made my stomach churn for a few minutes.

I let my legs buckle and carry me to the floor, wondering whether I would make it back to the settee before passing out.

I woke with Carl's blankets wrapped around me and no clear memory of making it out of the kitchen, let alone to the sofa bed. My teeth chattered so hard I wondered if they'd break against each other. My skin stretched too tightly across my chin. The light in the room blinded me. I closed my eyes and placed my hand over my forehead. My fingers were like ice and my head like fire. Checking one's own temperature was problematic at best, but I was certain I had a fever. I tried to sit up. Bile rose in my throat. It was no good. I just had to rest. I lay back on the damp pillow and remembered snippets from the past twenty-four hours. There had been dreams. Dark creatures expelled from my pores, slithering over my skin. Yolanda with a cold cloth pressed against my face, Carl holding a filthy tin bucket as far from his wrinkled nose as possible and hurrying out of the room. I called out, but nothing louder than a rattle came from my chest. My body was soaked as if from a deluge. My thighs slipped against each other as I tried to get comfortable.

Brief periods of bleary wakefulness surrounded by vivid dreams. In the dream world I explored the forest as bright eyes watched me from the shadows. I saw again the slow, heavy movements of creatures in the river, and I heard their siren call, telling me to join them. The sun rose and set and rose again. My body spasmed as countless black leeches pushed their way out through my skin, leaving me wet and sore.

Yolanda and Carl were there but not there. They cared for me and gathered what my body expelled. Changed soiled sheets and made me drink cups of cloudy water that tasted like lead. I was too weak to lift my hand and the drinking straw stuck to my scabby lips. I wished for death and was certain it would come for me soon.

The last time I woke I managed to sit up. My skin was cool and dry, not cold and clammy. The haze in the room was gone and I saw books, statues and discarded male clothing with perfect clarity. The sunlight, which nudged through the gap in the heavy curtains, didn't hurt my eyes. The fever had broken.

Carefully I stood up. My legs were weak from lack of use, but held me steady. Muscles ached as I stumbled to the door, but I did not fall.

I opened the door quietly and stepped into the bright kitchen. Yolanda was there, sat at the table with her laptop. She smiled.

'Hi Kate. How are you feeling?'

My knees buckled.

The pressure of her arm against my ribcage pulled me back. She was trying to lift me. I reached out to the panelled wall and supported my weight, pressed against her in an embrace, with my feet on the floor.

'I thought … '

'What did you think?'

'How long was I unconscious?' I asked.

'Most of the day. If you weren't better tomorrow we were going to get you to a doctor.'

'Just a day?'

'Are you hungry?'

'Thirsty,' I said.

'I'll get you some water.'

She helped me reach the table and I lowered myself onto a chair. She closed her laptop and filled a glass from a bottle in the fridge.

'Thank you.'

The water tasted so clear and fresh. It was as though I

had drunk nothing but sweat and sludge for weeks.

'Where's Carl?' I asked.

'Fishing.'

I nodded. None of it made any sense. Was it a dream? Slow and gentle, like an impressionist's rendition of a scene. Spots of light and only the idea of a kitchen, a friend, a table. I touched the table top and thought I felt wood, but distantly like a memory.

Yolanda pursed her lips. 'How are you feeling?'

I shook my head slowly, afraid that too swift a movement would send me away from this scene. 'You don't want to know. Any new photos?'

'I'm just working on yesterday's. I thought it best not to leave you alone.'

'I'm sorry.'

'No need. Maybe you ate something that didn't agree with you. You didn't drink the water, did you?'

I shrugged. Had I drank the tap water or just dreamed that I had?

'I thought I warned you. Sorry. We don't have drinking water. We don't even use the tap water to make coffee. Maybe we should take you into town and get you checked out.'

'I'll be fine.'

She touched my forehead and I thought I might weep. 'At least your fever has broken. Will you be okay for a minute if I go and tell Carl you're awake?'

'Just refill my glass first.'

As Yolanda left, I found myself staring at the cellar door again. Had it all been a dream brought on by bad food or toxic water? It had seemed so real: the noises in the cellar, Carl falling and my locking him in there, Yolanda's disappearance, the car driving away, leaving me behind, alone. It had all happened, hadn't it? It wasn't just a dream. Did that mean I was dreaming now?

I downed the delicious water and made my way across to the door. It was bolted again. I touched the cool metal and stood there for a moment, weighing my options. If I went down there what would I find? Could I prove to myself either way, whether Carl had been locked in the cellar? Whether we had even gone down there together?

I heard footsteps on the porch and returned to my seat.

'Katie!' Carl said smiling. 'Welcome back.' He didn't seem angry.

'When was the last time you saw me awake?' I asked.

He frowned. 'Dinner. You went to bed early.'

'We didn't go into the cellar?'

He shook his head.

My mind screamed, *liar!* But I couldn't trust my memory and why would Carl lie to me?

'Do you want me to take you to the doctor?' he asked and walked towards me, touching my forehead in the same gentle way Yolanda had before.

I shook my head and a fat tear pooled under my eye then rolled down my cheek.

'It's okay,' he said, clasping my hand. 'It was the fever.'

'Do you want to talk about it?' Yolanda asked. 'Your dream, I mean.'

My cheeks burned. I was ashamed as if I really had locked them both in the cellar and left them there. 'I just remember the cellar was really muddy, flooded.'

Carl searched my eyes for more, but I wasn't ready to offer it. That's it. If the cellar was muddy that meant it wasn't a dream.

'Can you show me the cellar?' I asked.

'Why?' Carl looked confused.

'So I can convince myself it was only a dream.'

Carl glanced over his shoulder at Yolanda who shrugged. 'Sure. If you want.'

'Will you come with me?' I asked.

He seemed a little nervous.

'Did you get locked in there? As a kid I mean. You look frightened.'

'How did you know that?' he whispered.

'What happened?'

'It was dark and I was scared. I thought ... '

'There was something down there with you?' I said.

He nodded slowly. 'I've never told … '

'Did it hurt you?'

Yolanda stepped forward and placed her hand on Carl's shoulder. 'Enough.'

'I'm sorry,' I said.

'Maybe you should go to bed.' Yolanda's stare was cold. Was she angry?

'I've slept enough,' I argued.

Carl drew away from me. Yolanda whispered something in his ear. He nodded. I didn't hear what she said, but it made me anxious. Carl glanced at me, frowning, then left.

Yolanda sat beside me. 'Tell me about your dream.'

I shook my head.

She sighed. 'Okay, you want to see the cellar?'

My skin crawled. I wasn't sure any more.

'Come on then.'

The light switch was the same as my dream, but the cellar was brighter when Yolanda switched it on. No longer just a dim puddle of light that barely reached past the end of the stairs, but a swathe of illumination that filled the small room. The floorboards were dry, not mud and concrete. I almost didn't bother to follow her down the stairs, until I saw something familiar in the corner. A tin bucket, the one Carl had carried from my room. Logically it probably contained my body waste, vomit or something else. The way he'd held it suggested a strong, unpleasant smell. But it was the only touchstone that connected my waking world with the fevered dreams and I wanted to take a closer look.

I followed Yolanda down the narrow staircase.

'See,' she said.

'Yes.' I walked towards the bucket.

'Kate?' Her voice was sharp.

'Just a moment.'

'I'm going back up.'

'Okay.'

Before the light went out I reached the bucket. It hadn't been emptied. Whatever I had expelled from my skin in the midst of my fever had grown. The black, slimy, over-sized leech-like creatures that curled around each other in the bucket were sleeping. At least until they smelled me. I saw their blind faces turn towards me just before everything went dark.

'No!' I screamed.

I ran towards the stairs, or so I thought, but I hit a wall. My toes sank into damp earth. Something heavy slid across my foot.

'Yolanda!' I shouted.

I heard the clatter of metal. A bucket pushed over, perhaps. They were coming for me. The flesh of my flesh. My nightmare.

My hands flailed in front of me as I ran away from the

sound. My foot slipped in the muck and I landed on my hands and knees. The room was silent other than my laboured breaths and I could not judge the direction of the stairs or the bucket. My body shook as panic took hold. When the first leech reached my toe I screamed then realised, too late, my mistake. They were everywhere, and now I had let them inside my mouth too. Their slimy noses pushed into every orifice. Even my tear ducts seemed a viable point of access, and they stretched and tore around the wet bodies. What I had dispelled in my fever were now forcing themselves back into my body. Racing like spermatozoa towards their goal.

My head swam as the dark stuff entered my brain. The others stopped moving inside me and those monsters, which were still outside my skin, made plopping sounds as they fell to the floor. I sat up slowly and realised it was light enough to see. The stairs were less than a metre away and I struggled towards them until the strength returned to my limbs and I was able to walk.

I had assumed the cellar door was locked, but the handle moved easily in my strong grip and I stepped into the bright kitchen, blinking. Yolanda was there, waiting. Her smile brighter than the sunlight. I walked towards her and she took my hand in hers, my skin, the shade of a bruise, deep purple, almost black, was much darker than hers now.

She led me out of the cabin and to the river bank

where Carl waited.

'She's ready,' Yolanda said.

Together we dived into the water, now the perfect temperature for a swim. Without moving her lips Yolanda told me everything was right. I would no longer be alone and my new family would take care of me. The truth of this wrapped me in a loving embrace and as my body sank deeper what was left of my mind soared high above, laughing.

The Violinist

Blood red. Black oblivion. Zipped up tight. Bright white. A whistled tune. Cold metal. So cold. Hard against her spine. Paralysed. Cold. So cold. Alone.

The dream returned again last night. It had the power of portent, but of what? Death? The tune Kel had recognised this time. One of Elizabeth's favourites: Mozart's Requiem.

Kel turned her head on the damp pillow and checked the clock on her bedside table. She'd slept through the alarm again. Another morning with her breakfast foregone and mismatched clothes hurriedly crawled into. No clean socks? The ones she wore the day before would do. Her nose crinkled as she sniffed. They didn't smell that bad.

The platform was crowded with commuters. Her slight frame weaved between bodies who cursed her impatience and poor etiquette. She leaped through closing doors in a way that had swiftly become her routine. Each morning she woke later. Eventually she wouldn't be able to regain lost time. One day she would be late, but not today.

Elizabeth Harper drew breath into her empty lungs. Frost burned her throat and set her chest on fire. Her naked back pressed against cold metal and a whisper of material clung to her face. Elizabeth was completely alone in the silent darkness.

The sheet fell from her as she sat up. Goose flesh prickled her skin and the darkness seemed absolute. A flicker of light from above, once, twice, before a fluorescent tube illuminated the room, humming like an angry insect.

Her eyelids were heavy, although there was nothing in her head to weigh them down. Her muscles ached. How long she had lain unconscious in this featureless room with only chilled air to keep her company? She tested her memory, but found no clue as to how or when she had got here. The fear that someone might return coaxed her into action and she swung her body around so that her toes reached the linoleum. For want of anything more substantial she wrapped the sheet around her body and risked sliding from the trolley, hoping her legs would be strong enough to support her weight. They shook in protest at first, but held her up and allowed her to stagger across the room to a double door. The handle clicked as she pressed down and the door opened into an office. Like before, the strip-light blinked twice before catching and shadows reached for her twice before they were banished by its brightness. She stepped through the doorway.

There was a small sofa here and a large desk. A desktop PC was switched off and a pile of papers balanced beside it patiently. A mug with a dark ring of old coffee grains, a Dictaphone, a key and a knife shaped letter opener sat to the right of the papers. Elizabeth lifted the letter opener, hoping it would suffice as a weapon should the need arise. Behind the desk stood a metal locker. Inside it she found a hospital uniform, the trousers too long and the buttonless shirt too baggy, but they were better than the sheet so she slipped them on. There was no mirror, but she assumed she must look clownish. Her short orange hair, red freckle-covered face and thin body swamped by the shapeless clothes.

The second door was locked. Her mind returned to the key on the desk, realising that it would be very lucky if it was the right one. Her luck held and the door opened inwards. She bit her bottom lip as she peered into the dark corridor and spotted an exit sign, glowing orange without the strength to highlight anything else around it. Shadows moved about the doorway. Taking a deep breath, she stepped out and a light flashed on once more.

The exit led to a stairwell. Perhaps she was in a basement as they led upwards only. Barefoot and afraid she ascended, clutching the makeshift knife in her fist. She tried again to piece together what had happened, but the last thing she remembered was the theatre. She had been playing her heart out and the audience had loved her. Strings had been breaking, scratching her cheek as she played. She tasted blood, and played harder. The moment she had worked towards for so long had arrived and perfection was within her grasp. Then darkness ... Then waking on the metal trolley ... But nothing between.

She reached a landing. Stairs continued upwards but the exit sign pointed towards a set of doors straight ahead. The lobby was not busy, but neither was it deserted. A receptionist ignored her and a nurse in green exited through a door on the left. A security guard sat sleepily beside a metal detector which waited between Elizabeth and the exit. The knife was heavy in her hand. Was it better to leave it here than risk being stopped, but what if she needed to protect herself? What if they wouldn't let her leave? She tucked the weapon into a crease at the back of a padded chair and hurried towards the exit. As she jogged through the metal detector she set off the alarm. The security guard and receptionist both glanced towards her, but neither rose from their seats or told her to stop. She kept going, out of the hospital and into the street.

Holding the trousers up at her thighs so her feet didn't tangle in the extra length, she ran away. She might not recall why she was in hospital, but at least she remembered where she lived. With no money for bus or taxi she walked quickly home. Stones and broken glass pierced her soles, but the pain didn't stop her. Once Elizabeth set her mind on something, nothing stopped her.

The ground floor of her apartment building was leased

as a massage parlour. When she arrived at the front door a sleazy looking youth opened it to leave and allowed her to slip inside without needing to buzz the superintendent. She climbed to the third floor. Yellow tape festooned her apartment door. Crime Scene. Had she been attacked here? She didn't remember anything like that, however hard she scratched the inside of her skull with her thoughts, trying to prise open her memory. There was no one here now. The door was locked, but she always stashed a key under the loose carpet at the end of the corridor and she retrieved it now. Her slender body limbo danced between the strips of tape and she entered her apartment, locking the door behind her.

Someone had trashed the place. Her cupboards and drawers hung open. The corner where her beloved instruments usually held court was empty. Cushions had been torn from her sofa and left scattered on the living room floor. Who did this? She fled to the kitchen but it was ransacked too. Bile rose in her throat. She swallowed hard as her eyes leaked saline. The bedroom too. She couldn't stay here. Even her sweet money bank, the piglet with a fiddle pressed under his snout was in pieces. Coins strewn across the floor. Elizabeth fell to her knees and wept. Her violins stolen and her home in ruins. Everything that made her life bearable was gone.

She would need to visit the police station, but for now

she was too tired and upset. She had no friends who would take her in. Her only choice was to sleep amid this carnage or book a hotel. She rushed to the bathroom. Had they found her hiding place? The flooring was intact. She prised up a vinyl tile and lifted the wood below. Her passport was there, cash and a new mobile phone, unused. She hadn't expected to need it so soon. At least no one else had discovered it.

The first twelve hotels she phoned were fully booked, but the thirteenth had a room. The taxi driver hadn't heard the name before so she gave him the full address. From the outside it looked more like a motel than a hotel, but she was used to squalid anonymity and too desperate for a soft bed and clean sheets to care. As she stepped through the front door of "Oletakers Hotel" she knew only relief.

Carpet with sickening green and orange swirls led to a mahogany reception desk. The place smelled damp and paper peeled from the walls, but the desk and the woman behind it dominated the vista. The woman watched Elizabeth with such intensity that she felt like a tightrope walker as she strode towards the desk. One wrong move and she might tumble into oblivion. She met the woman's stare, defiantly. Elizabeth Harper refused to be afraid of anything or anyone.

She had thought at first that the woman was standing, but as she reached the desk she realised this wasn't true. The woman was huge. How the stool beneath her didn't break was another mystery in a day full of them. It didn't surprise Elizabeth that the woman was black, this was a cosmopolitan part of the city. But the woman's beauty took her breath away. Her skin was a shade between caramel and burnished gold. A scarf was wrapped around her head, covering her hair, but Elizabeth imagined it would be thick and full of curls. Her lip curled in what resembled a proud but inquiring smile and her eyes were like inkwells.

'Welcome to Oletakers,' the woman said, completing her smile by uncovering perfect teeth. 'Do you have a reservation?'

There was the soft hint of a French accent in the woman's voice, which broke the painful silence like an aria. Elizabeth nodded, hardly trusting herself to speak. If she woke up in her apartment that moment from a vivid dream she would not be surprised. Everything around her seemed soft, obscured, unformed. Everything except the larger than life receptionist and those penetrating shark's eyes in that otherwise exquisite face.

'What is the name?' the woman asked.

Elizabeth handed her the passport.

The woman opened the leather bound document. She waved her hand over the page. One name vanished and another appeared in its place. Elizabeth shuddered as she watched the woman write the name Rebecca Black into the Guest book and the number 316 beside it.

Taloned hands passed the open book and fountain pen to Elizabeth for her signature. Elizabeth reached across too quickly and must have scratched herself on a fingernail. A few drops of bright blood hit the page and her face flushed as she apologised.

'It is no matter,' the woman assured her.

Hastily Elizabeth scratched the fake name onto the page and returned the book.

'Room three – one – six,' the woman said as she passed a leather fobbed key. 'Third floor.'

'Thank you,' Elizabeth said, heading towards a dark wood staircase.

'Miss Black,' the woman said.

Elizabeth turned.

'Have a restful night. Breakfast is served at eight.'

Police were sniffing around the theatre like hyenas when Kel arrived. One met her at the barrier.

'I work here,' she said. 'What's the problem?'

'Were you here yesterday?' the officer asked.

Kel nodded.

'What time did you leave?'

'Six.'

'Was the orchestra still here when you left?'

'They had a rehearsal. We open on Monday.'

He scribbled notes into the small hardback jotter.

'What's this about?' Kel asked.

'I'm sorry but I can't answer that question at the moment. You'll need to make a full statement. One of the detectives will be out in a moment. You can ask them your questions. What's your full name and what is your job here, Miss?'

'Ms. It's Kelly Frost. I work in the costume department. What's going on? Can I get to work?'

'No, Ms Frost. You can wait over there with your colleagues.' He pointed towards the box office and three of Kel's workmates hanging around just inside the barriers.

Mitchel was there. She hurried over to him. He looked away from her toward the theatre.

'Mitch, what happened here?'

He shrugged still not meeting her eyes.

'Are they going to let us in soon?'

'I think there's been an accident?' Suzie told her. 'I saw Mr Evans earlier and he looked white as a sheet. As if he'd seen a ghost.'

'Phantom of the fucking opera,' David said, scowling. 'Meanwhile we'll freeze out here. It smells like snow.'

'An accident?' Kel said. 'Who?'

'No one knows yet,' Suzie said. 'They're keeping very quiet.'

The double doors at the top of the marble steps opened and two paramedics exited the theatre carrying a heavy gully with a very full black plastic body bag on top.

'Shit!' Mitchel exclaimed.

Kel went to grab his hand but he shook her away.

'What the fuck happened in there?' Kel asked.

'Only the singers are that big.' David laughed darkly.

'Shit!' Mitchel said again.

'Heart attack?' Suzie suggested.

'Don't be stupid. We wouldn't need all these cops if someone had a heart attack,' David growled.

Suzie glared at him. 'Don't call me stupid, and don't pretend like you know what happened. Dickhead.'

'Don't call me that,' David said, encroaching on her personal space.

'What are you going to do? Poison my coffee, tea boy?' Suzie's smile was cold.

David glared like he wanted to hit her, but instead he slunk away and rested his back against the sandstone wall. He shook his head and pulled a cigarette from a crumpled packet. 'Bitch.'

'Calm down you two,' Kel said. 'We don't want another body in a bag.'

As if summoned by her words paramedics exited the theatre again with exactly that – another body in a bag.

Elizabeth tossed and turned all night. At the edge of her hearing she caught the sweet refrain of cello and flute. The music, while strange, was intensely beautiful. She drifted in and out of crimson dreams, calmed by the dark lullaby.

'Who was playing last night?' Elizabeth asked the delicately pretty Asian man who poured her coffee.

He looked confused.

'I heard music.'

'Oh yes. The band plays every night.'

'In this room?'

'In the residents' bar on the sixth floor.'

Elizabeth nodded. 'Thank you.'

'What would you like to eat?'

She thought for a moment. She couldn't remember the last time she ate and yet she experienced no hunger pangs. 'Just toast please.' She should try and eat something before she visited the police station.

The man bowed before he withdrew from the table. How strange? This place was like something out of an amateur opera, everything exaggerated to the point of ridiculousness. Yet again Elizabeth suspected she was dreaming.

The toast, when it arrived, tasted like ashes. She pushed it away and finished her coffee.

~

'Thank you for your patience, Ms Frost.' The detective gestured towards the empty leather chair that stood at a ninety degree angle to the one he occupied.

'What happened?' Kel asked.

'We'll come to that,' he assured her. His smile was professionally reassuring and she wanted to believe him. 'I've just got a few questions I need to ask you.'

Kel nodded. 'Yes, of course. Anything I can do to help.'

'So you work at the theatre?'

'Yes. I'm head costumer.'

'Were you working yesterday?'

'Yes. We're opening next week and I needed to make final alterations to some of the costumes. I left at six and headed home.'

'Where's home?'

'A twenty minute tube ride from here. Crown Gardens,' Kel replied. 'Can I ask about Elizabeth?'

'Elizabeth?'

'Elizabeth Harper. She's in the orchestra. She plays violin. She was here last night, practising. Is she okay?'

'Why do you ask?'

'I – I saw the body bags.'

'Was Elizabeth Harper a friend of yours?'

Kel nodded. Fat tears gathered in the corners of her eyes. *Was?* 'Is she dead?'

'How well did you know Miss Harper?'

Never as well as I wanted, Elizabeth thought,

picturing the red-haired pixie she'd watched day after day. 'We spoke a few times. Please tell me if she's okay.'

'There is some confusion about that. So you left at six and caught the train home, is that correct?'

Kel nodded, no longer able to see clearly through the moisture in her eyes.

'Do you live alone?'

Kel nodded again.

'And what time did you arrive home?'

Kel sniffed and wiped her face with her sleeve. 'Umm, about quarter to seven, I think.'

'Did anyone see you arrive?'

Kel stared at the detective, blinking away her tears so she could read his expression. 'Am I a suspect?'

'A suspect in what, Ms Frost?'

She shook her head. 'The body bags ... Was someone murdered? Do you suspect me?'

'We haven't ruled anything out at this point. We are simply gathering facts. Do you remember seeing anyone when you arrived home?'

'Ummm ... I called into the corner shop to buy a pint of milk.'

'Can you give me the name and address of this shop?' The detective passed his pad and a pen across to Kel and she scribbled down what she thought the name and address might be.

'Is that all?' she asked.

'Do you know of anyone who might have wanted to prevent the opening of the play next week?'

'Opera. Ummm ... No.'

'Are you aware of any arguments between members of the orchestra?'

'Other than the normal petty jealousies? No.'

'Was Elizabeth Harper jealous of anyone in the orchestra?'

'Of course not. She's very talented.'

'Was anyone jealous of her?'

'I don't know. I – I don't think so. No. She's quiet. She doesn't make enemies. You're asking a lot about Elizabeth. Please can you tell me what happened, or at least if she's in one of the body bags I saw being taken away?'

'She isn't in one of the body bags you saw being taken away.'

'Thank God!'

'I'm going to get someone to check that you were at ... Kurt's Corner Store, yesterday. I'll need you to wait with your colleagues until we want to interview you again.'

'Okay.'

'What did they ask you?' Mitchell asked as Kel hurried back to the group.

'Where's David?' she asked.

'They called him in after you. Fucking Dickhead,'

Suzie replied.

'Did they ask you about Elizabeth?' Mitchell asked.

'Yes, but they wouldn't tell me what happened.'

'We've been listening in and it seems six people are dead. Two singers and four musicians.' Suzie said.

'Elizabeth?' Kel asked.

Suzie shook her head. 'They haven't given any names. But apparently the singers got carved up.'

'It's horrible,' Mitchell said shaking. 'We saw them all yesterday. And what about the other musicians? Where are they? Where's Elliot? I rang, but I can't get an answer.'

'Did they treat you like suspects?' Kel asked.

Suzie's stare was hard. 'I had to give them my whereabouts last night, but I think it was just a formality.'

'Me too,' Mitchell agreed. 'Shocking. What's going to happen to the theatre? Will we lose our jobs? I just moved into a new apartment. I can't afford to be unemployed.'

Kel hugged him. 'Elliot will be okay.'

Mitchell rubbed his face. 'I'm sure Elizabeth is too.'

Elizabeth walked the four blocks to the police station. It seemed very busy. People were rushing about and no one paid her any attention. There was a queue for the only manned desk and she joined it, humming to herself.

She jumped when a hand touched her shoulder. The breath in her ear was icy and sent unnerving shivers up and down her spine.

'They can't help you,' the voice said.

She craned her neck to see a tall woman with black hair and violet eyes at her shoulder.

'What do you mean?'

'They are too busy with the theatre case. They don't care about your petty break in.'

'The theatre case?'

'Murder.' The woman nodded.

'My theatre?'

'We should talk elsewhere,' the woman said and walked toward the door.

After a moment's hesitation Elizabeth followed. The queue didn't seem to be moving anyway.

They sat in a café. Two steaming cups were already at the table. The woman picked up the one nearest to her and drank. Elizabeth reached across and touched her cold hand. 'We can't drink someone else's coffee.'

'They're ours,' the woman assured her. 'I'm Lucy. I'm your new best friend.'

Elizabeth shook her head and left the second cup alone. She moved to stand up but Lucy stopped her with a glare.

'Elizabeth, it's okay. I have your violin.'

'What?'

'It's back at the hotel.'

'How?' She shook her head again. *How did this stranger know her name? How did she know about the hotel? How did she have the violin? Did she break into the apartment?*

'Let's just say I'm your guardian angel. It's simpler to understand.'

'No let's hear the whole truth.'

'Are you sure?'

'Yes.'

'Well maybe we should have stronger drinks in that case.' With a flourish of Lucy's wrist the cups of coffee become tumblers of amber liquid.

'How?'

'Guardian angel.'

Elizabeth took a large sip that warmed her throat and chest. 'I'm ready.'

'It will be easier if I show you,' Lucy replied placing an index finger on each of Elizabeth's temples.

Elizabeth's body shook and she gasped in pain that ripped her chest. Tears fell from her wide eyes. 'No!'

Mitchell's mobile rang. 'It's Elliot,' he said, grinning. 'Hey sweetie. I was worried. Why didn't you pick up.' He nodded. 'Hang on,' he said and took the phone away from his face. 'They took him to the hospital for shock. He's been at the police station all night. But he's okay.'

'What happened?' Kel asked.

'Babes, what happened? We're outside the theatre now. The police have been questioning us.' Mitchell's eyes became unfocused and he nodded as he listened intently. His face blanched. 'Oh my God! No!' When he moved the phone away again he pressed his fingers to his trembling mouth.

'What?' Kel asked.

Mitchell shook his head.

'Tell us,' Suzie insisted.

'It's awful,' Mitchell said. 'I think I'm going to puke.'

'Can we get some water over here?' Suzie shouted as Mitchell doubled over, retching.

As the green shade faded from his cheeks Kel asked again. 'What happened?'

'We should sit down,' Mitchell said. 'You aren't going to like what you hear.'

'Elizabeth?'

Mitchell nodded. His face changed colour and he emptied the rest of his guts on the marble steps.

They moved away from the acrid smell and sat on an oak bench framed between pillars, where smokers usually congregated at break times. Mitchell sat in the middle and both women leaned toward him so as not to miss a word.

'It wasn't an accident,' Mitchell said.

Kel shivered. If the next word was Elizabeth she

would probably scream.

'Elizabeth murdered two singers, Roberto and Amelia.'

Kel shook her head. She wanted to laugh and she wanted to scream. 'What?'

'There was a small audience. Two people came up onto the stage mid rehearsal. One passed Elizabeth a knife. She carved out the singers' throats with it.'

'I don't believe it,' Kel said.

'What happened then?' Suzie asked.

'Someone in the crowd fired. They hit three other violinists before Elizabeth went down.'

'Elizabeth is dead?' Kel asked.

Mitchell nodded. Duty over, he broke down and wept into his lap. Suzie put her arm around him. Kel stood up. The world was spinning. She was trapped in a vortex. She staggered away from the bench and fell to her knees on the paving stones. She heard a shout then felt arms around her, lifting her. She opened her jaws and screamed.

The four members of staff were brought back to the makeshift interview room. David was there, pouting. The detective motioned for them to sit down. 'So as I understand it now you know as much as we do,' the detective said.

'Where is Elizabeth now?' Kel asked.

Mitchell frowned. He probably thought her obsession

was unhealthy, but fuck him. Elizabeth wasn't a murderer. There had been a mistake.

'She was taken to the morgue, but ...'

'But?'

'Her body has disappeared. We don't know who took it or why,' the detective said.

'Who were the people in the audience, the ones who gave her the knife?' Kel asked.

'We don't know. No one else there recognised them. Apparently one was a tall woman and the other a short man. We are checking out the CCTV to get a positive ID. There is one other thing ...'

'What?' Susie asked.

'We don't know why, but they took the singers' vocal chords with them.'

'But, I wouldn't ...' Elizabeth said. Her eyes held Lucy's stare, desperately. What she had seen couldn't be real.

'You were so much more talented than the rest of them. You were wasting away, undiscovered and unappreciated,' Lucy said.

Elizabeth nodded. 'But still ... I don't understand. What possessed me?'

'We all have two sides. One dark and one light. Nothing possessed you, but your other side.'

'They shot me. How am I? How am I still alive?'

'Well ... technically you're not.'

Elizabeth's jaw dropped.

'But that doesn't have to stop you. In fact it liberates you.' Lucy squeezed Elizabeth's hand. 'Don't you see? As Rebecca Black you can do so much more than Elizabeth Harper ever did.'

Elizabeth pulled her hand away and lifted her shirt. Four black holes pitted the skin of her stomach.

'They're bigger at the back.'

Elizabeth reached across her back and touched tendrils of cold flesh where her skin had once been.

'Two went straight through,' Lucy said, matter-of-factly.

'I don't understand.'

'You will. Just take it slow. When you're a newborn in your momma's arms you know nothing, but I will teach you.'

Elizabeth shook her head. The weight of this nightmare crushed her. She was either dreaming or insane.

'Let me take you home.' Lucy's voice was soft and soothing. It caressed Elizabeth's mind. She had no choice but to follow her back to Oletakers Hotel.

Weeks after the theatre massacre Elizabeth's body was still missing and Kel held tight to the thought that she was still alive. Opening night was cancelled, of course, but new musicians and singers had been engaged by the theatre and they were due to open in two weeks and already sold out. Tragedy attracted the public it seemed, especially well reported tragedy like this one.

After a long day of altering and sewing new costumes, Kel returned to her flat with nothing but a pint of milk to show for her trouble. The front door stalled over a pile of mail and Kel bent to pick it up. Bill, bill, funeral plan, a small red envelope with no stamp and only her name in beautiful script on the front. She carried it all to the kitchen, kicking the door closed behind her and eagerly ripped open the scarlet letter.

You are invited to Oletakers Hotel, tonight at 11pm, for the premier performance of Hades Wake.

Elizabeth.

Kel clutched the card to her chest. She was right. A quick search online told Kel where the hotel was and she rushed to the shower, whistling happily.

Dressed in her finest clothes, stomach fluttering like a school girl on prom night, Kel made her way to the hotel. From the outside it looked like a dump. The invitation assured her that the name was right and she jogged excitedly towards the reception desk. The beautiful black woman behind the desk told her to take the elevator to the sixth floor. It was 10.45pm.

The bar was dark and most of the faces unfamiliar, but

she saw Mitchell and Elliot at the bar and joined them.

'You got one too?' Mitchell asked.

Kel nodded.

'Were you tempted to show it to the police?' Elliot asked.

Kel hadn't even considered doing so. She shook her head.

'I told Mitchell to report it, but he was adamant he wanted to come. I guess I'm the bodyguard in this scenario. Or a gatecrasher. I still think we should have back up though. You weren't there. You didn't see what happened.'

The barman saved her from having to formulate a coherent reply and asked what she wanted to drink. 'Southern Comfort,' she said avoiding eye contact with Elliot.

'The stage is over there,' Mitchell said. 'Let's grab a table.'

As Elliot and Kel followed him, Elliot grabbed her hand but she shook it away. 'She's my friend,' she snarled.

Three empty chairs were arranged in a semi-circle on the stage. Kel sat mesmerised, cradling her drink, and staring at the chairs, willing Elizabeth to appear.

A tall woman with black hair and violet eyes approached the stage. Her dress was made of a fine purple velvet that seemed to swallow light.

'Tonight,' the woman said in a gentle voice that

somehow filled the room. 'We are proud to present our resident band with a new member. Please put your hands and hooves together for Hades Wake.'

The band must have sneaked onto the stage in her shadow, because as the woman moved away Kel saw the three seats had been filled and there was Elizabeth, violin at her chin, waiting to play.

Kel and Mitchell cheered. Elizabeth's concentration didn't break. Elliot got up and moved away from the table, but Kel was too entranced to care. Elizabeth was here. The red haired pixie who played like an angel. Everything was good in the world.

As Elizabeth's bow glided across the violin strings a strange sound echoed around the room. The sound of a weeping soprano. Kel's eyes filled with tears and she opened her soul to the music, letting it transport her to magical worlds of fairies and fawns. She danced naked in a forest under a golden moon. She twirled and spun like a dervish. Between the trees were the band, still playing with all their energy. But now Kel saw that the violin and cello were actually Amelia and Roberto, the dead opera singers, on their knees before Elizabeth and the cellist. The singers' throats were cut wide open. Elizabeth sawed back and forth with her bow, across Amelia's vocal chords, drawing splatters of blood from the grotesque instrument.

'We have to go,' a voice in her ear told her. In a land

far away Mitchell tugged at her elbow. She batted him away.

He'd pulled her back from the forest to the bar and there was Elizabeth, making the strangest and sweetest sounds on her violin. There too were the cellist and flautist. All were inside the music as though it was a bubble that separated them from the rest of the room. They didn't notice the shouting or the scuffling by the door. They didn't glance up as the SWAT team swarmed the room pointing pistols at the musicians. The air was full of white light and explosive cracks of sound. Something hard and hot hit Kel's chest and she drew her hands up to catch the blood flowing from her wound.

'Kel!' Mitchell shouted as he was pulled away by a man in uniform.

'Elizabeth,' Kel wheezed as she clutched her burning chest.

The pixie moved her delicate head. She caught Kel's stare and smiled back. Kel held onto that smile as she fell to the floor. *Blood red. Black oblivion. Zipped up tight. Bright white. A whistled tune. Cold metal. So cold. Hard against her spine. Paralysed. Cold. So cold. Alone.*

If you enjoyed this collection of short stories, please consider leaving a review with your favourite online book retailer.